GUYS READ

THRILLER

Also available in the Guys Read Library of Great Reading

VOLUME 1—GUYS READ: FUNNY BUSINESS

GUYS READ

THRILLER

EDITED AND WITH AN INTRODUCTION BY
JON SCIESZKA

STORIES BY

**M. T. ANDERSON, PATRICK CARMAN,
GENNIFER CHOLDENKO, MATT DE LA PEÑA,
MARGARET PETERSON HADDIX,
BRUCE HALE, ANTHONY HOROWITZ,
JARRETT J. KROSOCZKA,
JAMES PATTERSON,
AND WALTER DEAN MYERS**

WITH ILLUSTRATIONS BY
BRETT HELQUIST

WALDEN POND PRESS
An Imprint of HarperCollinsPublishers

Walden Pond Press is an imprint of HarperCollins Publishers.
Walden Pond Press and the skipping stone logo are trademarks and registered trademarks of Walden Media, LLC.

Library of Congress Cataloging-in-Publication Data is available.
ISBN 978-0-06-196376-6 (trade bdg.) — ISBN 978-0-06-196375-9 (pbk.)

Typography by Joel Tippie
11 12 13 14 15   LP/RRDB   10 9 8 7 6 5 4 3 2 1
❖
First Edition

CONTENTS

BEFORE WE BEGIN . . .

Why is that shady-looking character lurking in the dark alley? What's he doing with that crowbar? Is that something in his other hand? What is he doing? What has he done?

That is the mystery.

I'll bet the kid who just spotted him knows what he's up to.

There's not enough light from the street or the full moon to see the guy's face clearly. What if he turns? The kid will see his face. But he will see the kid. And then what?

That is the thriller.

You will have to work out the rest of the story yourself, because that's all we've got from Brett Helquist's cover.

And Brett is suddenly not talking anymore. Smart guy.

Welcome to Volume 2 of the Guys Read Library of Great Reading. Volume 1, *Guys Read: Funny Business* was all funny. Volume 2 is a crazy collection of mysterious, strange, scary, weird . . . and all thrilling. Which is why we are calling it *Guys Read: Thriller.*

We asked only the best thriller authors to write for this volume. I'm sure you know most of them, if not all of them. What you don't know is that these writers have delivered with the wildest mix of detectives, spooks, cryptids, snakes, pirates, smugglers, a body on the tracks, and one terribly powerful serving of fried pudding.

What happens next?

You read and find out.

And don't look now, but the guy in the alley is turning your way.

Jon Scieszka

THE OLD, DEAD NUISANCE
BY M. T. ANDERSON

"The psychics are having a huge argument," said Paul's dad. "Sit and read behind the sofa."

"There's mouse stuff behind the sofa," Paul complained.

"What do you mean by 'mouse stuff'? Tiny little lamps and suitcases?"

"Poo and weird hair."

"Just hide somewhere. Stay out of the shot."

Paul's dad was the cameraman for a show called *True Spook*. They were filming at a house that was supposed to be haunted. Paul had to keep out of the way in case one of the psychics swept past, calling out the names of the dead or saying she felt cold spots near the credenza.

"All right," muttered Paul, taking his book of world records and crouching behind a side table. "Is this hidden enough?"

"Roger that," said his father, giving a thumbs-up. "We're probably not coming into this room. No one's heard or seen anything in here. I'll give a shout when the coast is clear." He hoisted his camera onto his shoulder and went to film the psychics' argument.

Paul looked around the room. Everything was old and ugly. The sofa was smelly and sixties. There were several TV trays with scenes of moose and ducks in the wild, standing in grasses. He picked up an ugly, three-legged ceramic plant holder filled with plastic flowers and put it on the table to hide him better, in case one of the psychics came in and had to be filmed hooting about ghostly presences. Paul didn't want to be in their way.

Each week, the *True Spook* team went to a different haunted place: a house; a cemetery; a dark, rusty factory; or even an old railroad bridge. They investigated the haunting. They filmed interviews of people who described what they'd seen.

Paul didn't believe a word of it. He thought it was suspicious that so many of the haunted places were inns that needed some publicity and restaurants where the rugs smelled weird. But it didn't matter how ridiculous the story was: once the *True Spook* team shot their footage and an editor cut up the interviews and pasted them back together again, and once a composer created creepy, groaning music to go along with the footage of fallen walls and spiders spinning in the eaves, it seemed like the story was absolutely true and the streets of America were packed with the dead, like a bunch of grim joggers.

Paul had just read about the record for the world's largest pie when one of the psychics stormed into the room. Her name was Louise. She stood for a moment, shook her arms, closed her eyes, and exhaled. Her head was back. She waited for a minute. She looked irked. Then she yelled into the hall, "We might as well leave. I can't feel anything in here. She's blocking my psionic extensions."

"I'm not blocking anything," said Phyllis, the other psychic. "Maybe you don't have enough powers."

"I have plenty of powers."

"Maybe you don't have enough powers."

"I said, I got plenty of powers."

"Hey, hey!" said the director, coming up behind Phyllis. "We're going to take a break. Louise, you go in there and try to settle down. Phyllis, you go in the dining room and try to—you know, open up a channel or something. To the afterlife. We're going across the street to the graveyard."

Paul's dad poked his head into the room. "Paul?" he said. "You want to come out to the graveyard?"

Paul nodded and unfolded himself from behind the side table.

Louise startled a little, then smiled at him. "Look at you. Hiding in here." She chuckled. "You could've give me a fright."

The other psychic yelled, "Not if you were psychic."

Louise bawled out, "Are you saying I'm not psychic?"

"I'm saying picking up on an actual, living kid doesn't take a large amount of powers."

"He was behind the side table. Under fake plants."

Paul left the house as quickly as possible.

Out in the graveyard, they were filming the host, the main ghost detective. His name was Dennis. He wore a long, black coat and a black suit, and he liked to look searchingly into the distance. He was a very dramatic person. He stood by a large funeral monument—an obelisk—and tried to arrange his hair to look mysterious.

It was a cold day out, and dirty snow lay on the ground. It was already trampled along the paths through the graveyard.

"Tell me when you're ready," said the director.

Dennis squinted. He didn't say anything. He just nodded.

"Action," said the director.

Paul's father zoomed in on Dennis, who drew a breath and said, "A cruel father. Bitter sons. A house filled with their spirits. A mysterious gravestone. This time on *True Spook*: 'The Family that Stays Together.'"

He paused, then lay his hand on the smooth side of the stone obelisk. "Here lies . . . a tragic story. The year is 1884; the place is the little town of Canaan, Massachusetts. A wealthy man, Josiah Smitch, dies. He has made a fortune in the China trade. But after his death, no one can find his money. It appears that, as a cruel prank, he hid it somewhere in his house. His sons are penniless. They tear the house apart looking for their father's fortune after his death, but they never find a single coin. They all die poor. Their only revenge . . . is this stone. . . ." Dennis patted the obelisk.

Paul's dad panned the camera up to film the words carved in marble.

Here lies
THE OLD NUISANCE
1806–1884

Dennis, the host, was staring off into the distance, as if unknown figures were beckoning him. In fact, Paul noticed, he was looking down the street at a gas station.

Dennis swiveled his intense gaze back toward the camera lens. "And now, both Josiah Smitch and his sons may walk the halls of his old house, still feuding." Dennis stared for a long time. Then the director said, "And cut." Paul's dad stopped filming. Dennis ate some Tic Tacs.

Paul asked him, "So where did the treasure end up being?"

"Uh-eh-uh," said Dennis, to the tune of "I don't know," while shrugging his shoulders. "Tic Tac?"

Paul took his Tic Tac carefully. He was not interested in ghosts. But he was very interested in treasure. He held the Tic Tac between his teeth and snapped it in half.

The crew did some other takes of the show's introduction with tangled, black trees in the background. They caught some sounds of dripping. They filmed tombs covered in icicles.

By now, Paul was eager to get back inside the house. Even though he knew it was silly, he daydreamed about finding the fortune hidden undiscovered for a hundred and twenty-five years. He wanted to fiddle with the banisters.

As they crossed back over the road to the house, Paul asked his father, "Do you think the treasure's still there?"

His father said vaguely, "Who knows?" He was thinking about exterior shots of the house surrounded by its bedraggled weeping willows.

Paul asked him, "What's the haunting like? When people say they've heard things? Where does it happen? What rooms and stuff?"

His father said, "Dining room. Where the Old Nuisance used to fight with his sons at dinner. Supposedly, you can still hear all of them yelling at each other sometimes. The old guy accusing them of things. Everyone really angry. Then there's the staircase. Josiah Smitch has been seen at the top of the stairs, dressed in black. The owners hear him screaming down the steps at his family. . . . And, uh, the worst is the bedroom where he died. No one will sleep there anymore. Not guests or anything. When the owner had some friends stay there, they woke up in the middle of the night, surrounded by frowning faces peering down at them. A circle of the guy's sons, waiting for their father to die. Pale faces, floating in the air around the bed."

"Wow," said Paul. "I bet the gold is still hidden in one of the haunted rooms."

"Maybe." Paul's father reached over and squeezed Paul's shoulder. "Don't tell me you're planning on finding the Smitch fortune."

Paul got a little embarrassed, because that was exactly what he wanted to do.

When they were back in the house, the owner, Mrs. Giovetti, came out of the kitchen to give the psychics a tour. She was a little old lady who had bought the house and some of its furniture from Josiah Smitch's granddaughter. She and her dogs had often seen the ghosts. She left the dogs in the kitchen, because they were terrified of the upstairs.

The psychics hadn't heard anything about the history of the house. They weren't allowed to, because then they wouldn't have to be psychic to figure things out. Now the whole group went from room to room, and the psychics talked about all their paranormal feelings. The idea was to film them, in case they saw something that sounded like Josiah Smitch or his sons.

Paul was very happy to get a chance to look around the old place. He followed the group carefully, hoping that if he stayed out of the shot, no one would complain. He saw the whole place. Most of the original walls had been covered in awful wallpaper—some of it striped, from the seventies, some of it with little fruit baskets, from the sixties. None of it had been fixed up for thirty or forty years. There was the dining room where Josiah Smitch had yelled at his sons during supper. The original table and chairs were still in the room, nicked and scratched. There was a battered Chinese screen with peeling painted birds. The psychics felt nothing. Then there was the staircase where the father had been seen screaming down at his children, dressed in black. The psychics said they got a vague sense of evil. They jostled each other to be the first up the steps. And upstairs, there was the bedroom where Smitch had died. The original bed was there, dusty and unused.

While Paul's dad filmed the bed, Phyllis, the more heavily perfumed of the two psychics, said, "I'm getting something in here." She quivered her fingers around in the air like beating wings. "Oh, yeah, someone's in here with us right now. . . . A young man . . . black hair. Kind of a black mustache. He's telling us to get out. He really wants us to leave. He says it's his house."

Dennis, the host, turned to the camera. "The psychics have not been told the history of the house. Whatever they pick up is just the result of their powers." He asked Louise, the other psychic, "Are you seeing this man, too?"

Louise closed her eyes. "Yes," she agreed. "He's with us. He says he's looking for a girl. . . . Her name is . . . two syllables. . . . Maybe Sharon?"

"That's not true," said Phyllis. "Actually he left the room a minute ago."

"He didn't leave. I just heard him talk about Sharon."

"Nope, he told us to leave the house and then he just walked out into the hall. I'm following him." Phyllis left the room with her hands outstretched, singing out, "Don't worry, spirit! At least I can see you!"

"He's still . . . he's still here," Louise claimed, but it didn't look like anyone believed her. Dennis left, so Paul's father left, and the director left.

"Hey! Hey!" complained Louise, and she followed them all out.

That left Paul alone in the room.

The others were arguing out in the hall. They tromped down the haunted steps.

Paul was the only person upstairs.

He looked around carefully, then poked the bed. He squeezed the mattress. It would be the perfect place to hide money. Then old Josiah Smitch would be lying right on top of it as he died. No one could take it without him knowing.

The mattress felt kind of normal. Paul was disappointed. He knew that old-time mattresses were supposed to be lumpy, since they were usually filled with corn husks or old feathers. He thought that probably this mattress was new. Only the bed frame was old.

Then Paul heard a rattle on the window, a tap.

He looked up.

The sky had gotten dark, and sleet was falling. It hit the panes with a tiny ping. The black branches outside in the yard bobbed up and down. Through them shone the dirty light from the gas station.

Paul went back to the examination of the bed. He squeezed the pillows. They didn't feel old, either. They felt like foam.

He looked around the rest of the room. He wasn't good at telling whether furniture was old or new. He figured a lot of the stuff in the room was newer, maybe from just twenty or thirty years before: a white dresser and a couple of lamps.

He sat on the bed. The sleet still struck the window.

A face was looking at him. It hung in the air. It glared.

Paul yelped. The eyes were huge. The mouth was down-turned. It hung there like a mask.

He looked wildly around—hoping that he'd see something that might be reflecting.

There were other faces. They also hung in the air. Brothers. They hated him.

Paul thought he should run to the door. But he couldn't. He didn't know why, but he couldn't move his legs or arms. Too terrified.

The faces hung all around him, staring down at the bed. Their eyes were like onions. Their lips moved. They spoke things Paul could not hear. Terrible things.

There was no sound of sleet anymore, or of the TV crew downstairs. Paul could hear a high, metallic ringing in his ears, but nothing else.

He threw himself off the bed with all his might. He raced for the door, hurled it open, and thundered down the steps.

Right into the middle of the shoot.

He smacked into the psychics.

"Oh, great," said Phyllis. "Thanks. There goes my ectoplasm."

"Honey," Louise complained, frowning at Paul. "We were just about to find out who the mysterious Sharon was, in olden days."

Paul heaved with deep breaths.

"There's guys in the bedroom!" he said. "I saw their faces! It's real!"

Phyllis rolled her eyes. "Now everyone wants in. Look, whoever you are—"

"He's my son," said Paul's father. "Sorry about this."

Phyllis nodded. "Well, why don't you take him outside. And Louise, let me tell you, once and for all, there isn't no Sharon."

"There is too!"

The psychics were off again. Thankfully, Paul's father

took him into the living room.

"They said we should go outside," Paul repeated.

"It's sleeting."

"I want to get out of this house. I saw guys upstairs."

"I wish you did," said Paul's father. "I can't stand working on this show sometimes. How can anything haunt us when we're all making so much noise?" He put down his camera and ran his fingers through his hair. "That's the problem with modern life. Too loud for ghosts."

"Can I sit in the van?"

"No. It's too cold out."

"It's not so cold."

"It's sleeting. We're going to be hours in here. Sit tight. Stay out of sight. I'm going to tell Dennis about your encounter and see if he wants to use it. No, never mind. What am I saying? I'm not going to let them interview you. Just stay here and for"—he checked his watch—"an hour and half, don't have any paranormal experiences. Roger that?"

"Roger that," said Paul unhappily.

His father picked up his camera and went back into the hall.

Paul stared at the door. He didn't want to be left alone. He had just seen ghosts. How was he supposed to sit here reading? Especially when, at any moment, psychics could burst in and tell him to move or to hide behind the table and the plastic plant?

To kill time, he decided to look for secret doors. He went around the room, knocking quietly on the walls to see if any of them were hollow.

He stopped that when he heard Louise, from the other side of the wall, say, "I hear knocking! Knocking! I'm here, Sharon! She has a bow in her hair! Knock again! Come on, honey! You can do it!"

He sat down behind the table and hid his head with the ugly green planter and the plastic flowers. He opened his book of world records and tried to read.

The house was silent. There was a distant ticking, that was all. He flipped a few pages.

Boring. Exciting at other times, but boring right now, when there was a fortune to find.

He poked his head up.

And found everything had changed.

The world outside the window was black, not gray. The ugly floral wallpaper was gone. The eighties furniture was gone. The room was restored to its old look, with ancient, stuffed chairs and a fireplace in the wall. There was no fire in the fireplace, though, despite the cold.

Instead, the wood was sheeted with ice, and something black dripped from the chimney. The flowers in the ugly green plant holder were dead.

Paul got a very bad feeling.

He crept to the door and opened it.

The hall with the staircase was bleary, as if his eyes wouldn't focus. He saw shadows flicking back and forth on the landing above him.

He didn't know what had happened. He wondered if he was dreaming. Or if this was a special kind of haunting, and he was walking into some ghostly trap.

He creaked down the hallway. And then, finally, he found himself in the dining room.

Once again, Mrs. Giovetti's awful wallpaper was gone. Instead, there was different awful wallpaper. The table and chairs were now new. There were portraits on the walls. The table was set for a meal with fine china and knives and forks and candles.

The candles were out. All of the plates had been smashed, and were in pieces at their place settings.

All except for one plate. At the head of the table. And sitting at the head of the table, facing away from Paul, was an old man with white, white hair.

Paul stared at the old man's back. It rose and fell with

ragged breathing. That was the only sound in the room, other than the ticking of the clock.

The man's head began to turn.

Paul panicked. He backed up.

The man was rising from his seat.

Paul scrambled to get back to the hallway—but he remembered the flickering shapes there, too.

The man turned. It was, apparently, Josiah Smitch. His face was square and sad, with heavy lines around the mouth.

"Young sir," hissed the ghost. "Your mediums are pelting me."

Paul had no idea what the ghost was talking about.

"The women who are trying to communicate. They are an irritation. Like someone ringing a servant's bell without cease. I do not come when called."

Paul shook his head a little. He didn't want the ghost to get mad.

But a thought struck him: this would be a really, really good time to talk to the dead guy about his fortune.

Carefully, he said, "Josiah . . . Smitch?"

"Yes, boy."

"It's, uh, great to meet you. We're making a whole show about you."

"A show? I pray there are no musical numbers."

"It's not that kind of show."

"Hallelujah. I cannot abide dancing girls."

"It's a show about you and your sons, and how they carved 'The Old Nuisance' on your tombstone and everything. And then, you know, you hid your treasure."

Josiah Smitch wobbled for a second. He turned back to the table and surveyed the smashed porcelain. "That's what they're saying, is it?" he whispered.

"Yeah," said Paul. "That's what I heard."

The old man turned back to Paul. He sniffed, long and hard. Paul realized that the dead man was trying not to cry.

Smitch raised his hand, and the walls faded. Somehow, Paul could see into the bedroom, even though it was upstairs. And old Smitch was not just standing by Paul; he was also lying on the bed, dying, while his sons were gathered around him.

The old man, lying in his nightgown, croaked and coughed to his sons, "I have tried to make you better men. I have sought to teach you of industry and work and generosity. Until I know that you shall not squander my fortune, I shall not tell you where I have hidden it. I do this only . . . only because you are my own dear sons. . . . You are, you know, my own dear sons . . . and when I am gone, you are the only ones who will remember me." His voice got very wet and fond, and he began choking on tears. He reached out to his sons with one clawlike hand—but none of them took it.

One son rolled his eyes.

Another whispered, "Let the old nuisance talk on. In a few hours, it'll all be ours anyway."

Then Paul saw the eyes of the old man on the bed. They were fixed on the son who'd spoken. He had heard. Paul could almost feel the old man's sorrow and anger, here in his last minutes.

Suddenly, the walls appeared again. The old man was standing by Paul's side. "A few hours later," the ghost whispered, "I called upon my lawyer to change my burial arrangements. My sons were not the ones who put 'The Old Nuisance' upon my gravestone. I ordered it put there myself. Imagine how they gasped when it was unveiled." He smiled. "And when they realized they would have to work for their money."

"So, um, where did you hide it? The money. Who finally got it?"

"Oh, nobody got it. It's still in the house."

"You know, where?" asked Paul, kind of offhandedly.

"I can't tell you," said the man. "Because of them."

And now Paul saw more spirits, growing thicker like

mist, each one sitting in a seat at the table, slumped over, facedown upon the broken plates.

As they clarified in the air, one by one they lifted their heads up and stared at him.

Paul was getting scared. Their eyes were large and their mouths unfriendly and they rose to trap him there at their feast.

Old Josiah Smitch said to Paul, "The answer was right in front of your face."

But his sons were swiping at the old man, disturbing him as if he were smoke. He billowed out to the side, closing his eyes sadly. The ghosts clawed their way toward Paul.

Paul scampered to the side, toward the door into the kitchen—no, the way was blocked by brothers.

He ran to the other side of the table. They drifted through the furniture toward him. He bolted out the door into the hallway.

The hallway was like it had been in the nineteenth century. Chinese lacquer paintings of beautiful women with tiny feet hung on the walls. Ghost sons and brothers were mobbing all the stairs and doors, their eyes dead set on Paul, their hands outstretched.

He tumbled into the room where he'd been hiding. There he was—in the same room he'd squatted in, but different, with different, old furniture, except—

No time to think . . . The ghosts were stepping in behind him.

But I know, he suddenly realized, and said out loud, "I know where the fortune is hidden! I know where he hid it!"

The ghosts stopped for a second, astounded.

Paul hurled himself into the middle of them.

As he passed through them, he caught the chill rush of centuries moving all around him. He saw his father and the psychics as if they were ghosts. He saw the camera and the modern furniture. He saw the nineteenth century passing away.

And then he was wobbling in the center of the floor by the foot of the stairs, looking into the living room, where he'd hidden earlier. The two psychics were standing in there, screaming at each other.

Phyllis was yelling, "There was no girl named Sharon!"

Louise was yelling, "Says who?"

"Says me!"

"Well, I heard her knock on the wall!"

"Hey," Paul interjected. "I think I know where the fortune is!"

Phyllis screamed at Louise, "You have no psychic powers!"

"Oh, yeah?"

"You heard me!"

"Once I contacted King Richard the Lionhearted!"

"I wouldn't trust you to phone for a pizza!"

And hearing that insult, Louise snapped. She let out a weird, animal yowl.

"Excuse me," said Paul, "but I just figured out that the ugly, three-legged—"

Louise picked up the ugly, three-legged flowerpot with the plastic flowers in it—*"No!"* said Paul—and smashed it over Phyllis's head.

The pieces went everywhere.

There were plastic peonies all over the rug.

The two psychics breathed heavily and stared at each other.

"Okay, Louise," Phyllis growled, tapping her forehead. "Can you tell what I'm thinking right now?"

Paul fell to his knees. He was surrounded by shards of pottery.

"It—it was the fortune!" he said. "The ghost told me that the fortune had been right in front of my face. And then, I saw that this flowerpot was here, even in old times. Josiah Smitch was in the China trade. I bet that this was some . . . some expensive Chinese piece of pottery."

Paul's father picked up a piece of heavy, green clay. "Like a Ming vase?"

"Not Ming. Shang," whispered a voice. It was the ghost

of Josiah Smitch. He was sitting next to Paul, apparently invisible to everyone else. He looked glum. "Much older than Ming," he said. "Priceless."

"Are you sure it's Ming?" Dennis asked Paul. "It looks kind of ugly."

Mrs. Giovetti explained, somewhat unhelpfully, "I used it to hold fake flowers."

"Not Ming," Paul muttered. "Shang."

They all turned in surprise to look at him.

Josiah Smitch, invisibly, nodded.

The psychics looked ready to argue.

But then again, now Paul, apparently, was a psychic too.

The ghost sighed. He quoted, "'He heapeth up riches, and knoweth not who shall gather them.'" Then he shrugged and walked through a wall.

Paul, young psychic, turned to the others. They were all staring at him. He had to say something.

Shang. Ming. Whatever. It was going to be a long day.

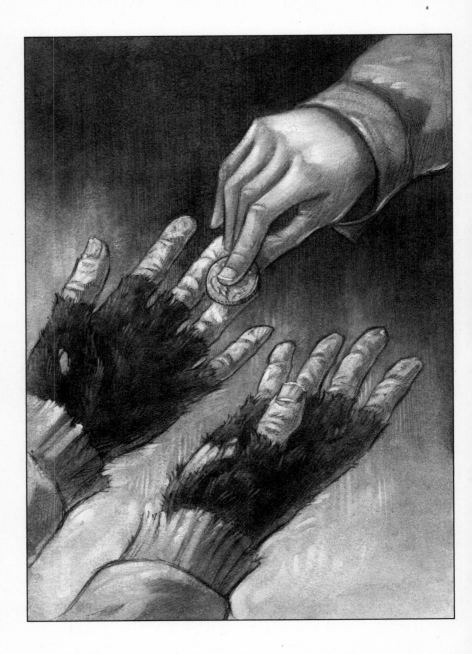

BELIEVING IN BROOKLYN
BY MATT DE LA PEÑA

"**O**r what if there was a wish machine on your wall?" Ray said, snatching the bag of generic-brand chips off Benny's mattress and pushing a grubby hand inside.

Benny frowned at his friend. "What are you talking about, 'a wish machine'?"

"Like, imagine that rig was built right into the house, B. And only kids knew how to use it. Be sick, right?"

Benny rolled his eyes and shrugged. He was over the stupid invention game Ray always wanted to play. What was the point? It wasn't like any of Ray's schizo ideas could actually come true.

A wish machine . . .

In somebody's wall . . .

No wonder the guy was barely passing seventh grade.

Ray wasn't done, though. "Wouldn't even have buttons, man. You'd just walk up to it and—"

"Dude, could we talk about something else?" Benny interrupted.

"I'm saying, though," Ray said. "You'd just walk up to it and whatever you thought in your head would come sliding out the slot. Like a Coke machine. Only nobody would think Coke, man, 'cause that's lame compared to other things you could think up."

Benny waved Ray off and snatched back the bag of chips. He poured the last few salty crumbs onto his tongue and swallowed. "Good luck with that," he said, wiping his mouth with the back of his hand. "I guess you still put cookies out for Santa, too, right?"

They were both sort of laughing now, Benny play-punching Ray in the ribs and Ray fending him off.

Soon they were talking about Ray's other favorite subject. Girls. More specifically, Sylvia Lawson, a neighborhood basketball star's little sister. Ray had been passing notes back and forth with Sylvia every afternoon during history. According to Ray, they were now talking face-to-face a little, too. Between classes.

"Yo, she wants to meet at the movies on Sunday," Ray said, giving himself a couple congratulatory thumps on the chest with the heel of his hand.

"Ronny know about this?" Benny said.

"Like I care."

Benny shook his head. "Bet you start caring when he's all up in your face. Dude's twice your size."

"Why's it gotta be anybody's business, B? We're talking about a PG movie."

Benny waved off his friend and peeped the clock. Almost eight.

Ray looked, too, and rolled his eyes. "I'm too grown to have some stupid curfew anymore." Still, he zipped open his backpack and shoved his remedial math book inside and zipped it back up.

Benny stood. "Hang on a sec and I'll walk you out."

When he came back from the bathroom he found Ray taping a piece of notebook paper to his bedroom wall, right above the hollowed-out fireplace. "Come on, man," Benny said, "you know my grandma trips about the wall-paper."

"It's just Scotch tape," Ray said. "It barely even sticks."

Benny stared at Ray's stick-figure drawing of a machine.

The crooked caption read: MAGICAL WISH MACHINE. He laughed a little and shook his head, told Ray he had emotional problems.

They walked out into the living room, both waving to Benny's sick grandma, who was slumped into the old couch, all bones and perm, watching the news on their tiny TV.

"All right, Mrs. Garcia," Ray said.

"Pull up them pants, Raymond," she snapped. "At least try and look like a human being."

She turned to Benny and Ray, coughing a little, and smiled her old lady smile. Benny watched Ray smile back, uncomfortably, and pull up his sagging jeans.

"Wait till I mention about the wallpaper," he told Ray under his breath.

They gave a quick fist bump, then Ray was out the door and Benny went over and sat next to his grandma, even though he hated watching news.

That night Benny couldn't sleep. He tossed and turned, thinking too hard. About the standardized test he'd have to take to get into a decent high school. About the Brooklyn hoop tournament he didn't sign up for this season. About Sylvia's friend Julie, who he still hadn't talked to, even though she was only three lockers down and occasionally shot him flirty looks.

But mostly Benny thought about his sick grandma, asleep in the next room. He imagined her chronic lung problem as a street gang of microscopic bugs that had crawled in through her ear one morning while she sat on the stoop sipping her sweet coffee. After a long march through his grandma's larynx and windpipe the bugs had settled in her lungs, where they continually tagged her organ lining with miniature cans of spray paint, making it impossible for her to breathe regular.

On cue, he heard his grandmother start coughing again in the next room.

What would he do if something happened to his grandma? He couldn't even think about it without feeling a hole opening in his stomach.

Benny sat up and rubbed his eyes and looked at the clock. Past midnight. He counted how many hours until he had to be up for school. Then he pulled off his blanket and went for his Game Boy.

On his way to the closet, though, he found himself standing in front of the lopsided drawing Ray had taped above the fireplace. He grinned a little thinking how people who were crappy at one thing, like Ray with school, were supposed to be decent at something else. For Ray, though, that "something else" definitely wasn't art.

Man, Benny thought. Was Ray good at anything? Girls maybe. But it wasn't like you had to do anything to be good at girls, right? Some people just had it like that.

Then Benny did something out of character.

He leaned toward the schizo drawing and thought, *My wish is for earplugs I could wear at night. So no microscopic bugs could sneak in with their spray-paint cans.*

Just thinking it, though, didn't seem official enough so Benny said it, too. "I wish for earplugs I could sleep with. Got that, Mr. Santa Claus? Earplugs."

He cracked up at himself and grabbed the Game Boy from the closet and played his outdated war game on mute. After two or three games he paused it for a sec to rest his eyes and fell asleep sitting up.

Benny woke up the next morning with a stiff neck. He climbed out of bed bleary-eyed and dragged himself to the bathroom to shower. As he walked back into his room he spotted something odd and stopped in his tracks.

The cracked stool he kept stored in his closet was now shoved inside the fake fireplace, right beneath Ray's wish machine drawing. On top of the stool was a pair of headphones he'd never seen before.

Benny picked up the phones and looked them over. Sonys that covered the entire ear. The initials JB etched into the right side. They weren't earplugs, but they were definitely in the same ballpark. Which was really weird. He glanced at Ray's drawing, then back at the headphones, then he spun around expecting to see Ray at the door, laughing. But there was nobody.

Benny dressed and got his book bag together and went into the living room, where his grandma was cackling at something on *The Today Show.*

"Hey, Grams," he said. "Did Ray stop by when I was in the shower?"

She turned to him, frowning. "You think I'd let that little hoodlum in here unsupervised?"

"Was anybody here? Did Auntie Rosa bring groceries early?"

"Nobody was here, Benny." She covered her mouth as she coughed. "At least nobody who still walks among us."

The sicker his grandma became, the more she spoke about ghosts. Sometimes she even talked to Benny's grandpa in her room. With the door closed. Even though he'd been gone over twenty-five years. Just a week ago he'd heard her sniffling through the door, explaining to her dead husband that she'd lost the silver chain he'd given her on their last anniversary together.

Benny considered that.

Maybe the ghost of the grandpa he'd never met was messing with him. Then Benny remembered a very important fact: he didn't believe in ghosts, or wish machines.

He held out the headphones, said, "By any chance, Grams, did you leave these in my room?"

She put on her reading glasses to see what he was holding. "Boy, you'd have to put me in a full hazmat suit to touch them feces-looking things." She slipped off her glasses and turned back to *The Today Show*.

Benny stared down at the headphones trying to figure out how they looked like feces.

On his way home from school that day, Benny ran into Ronny and Simón on Seventh Avenue. They were coming out of a bodega with their daily Twinkies and strawberry Nesquiks, and when they spotted him, Simón held out a fist and said, "B Man."

Benny tapped Simón's fist. Then Ronny's.

"Spare a little change?" a pencil-thin homeless man said, rattling the coins in his old Styrofoam coffee cup. He was sitting on an overturned bucket outside the store, his usual spot, and he looked like death.

"Nah, old man," Simón said.

"You don't need change," Ronny said, "you need a bar of soap."

When the guys turned and started walking, Benny slipped the homeless dude a couple quarters. Like he always did. Not because Benny was some great guy. But because this skinny old beggar, for whatever reason, made him think of his grandma. And whenever he thought about his grandma, sick at home, while he was out hanging around, he felt guilty, like he owed somebody something.

They cruised Seventh Avenue, Ronny and Simón unwrapping their Twinkie packs and Benny looking more closely at the headphones around Ronny's neck. They were Sonys. Same model as the ones he'd found in his room. Ronny's initials weren't JB, they were RL, but it still seemed like a crazy coincidence.

"So it's true what I heard?" Ronny said.

"What?" Benny said.

"Your boy's trying to talk to my sis?"

"Who, Ray?" Benny said.

"You ain't gotta lie to kick it," Simón said. "Sylvia's been, like . . . developing, man."

Ronny looked at Simón.

Simón shrugged and sipped his strawberry milk.

"I think they're mostly friends or whatever," Benny said.

"He doesn't think he's some big baller?" Ronny said.

"No way," Benny said. "He's too busy trying to make it out of seventh grade."

Simón smiled a little.

Ronny didn't.

They were all quiet for a bit as they continued walking, Benny spying the serious look on Ronny's face. He was two years older. A freshman. Already the star power forward on John Jay's varsity hoop squad. Benny thought how weird it was to see such a powerful-looking dude rocking a pink milk mustache.

"Yo, Sylvia's irritating," Ronny said. "And those bangs she got make her look like a Chihuahua."

Simón laughed.

"But tell your boy Ray," Ronny said, "if he messes her over I'm gonna have to stomp him out."

"Ray won't mess nobody over," Benny said. "I promise."

"Yeah?"

Benny nodded.

Simón opened a second Twinkies pack and handed one of the greasy yellow loaves to Ronny, who broke it in half. He held the shorter end out to Benny, and Benny took it.

"It's all good," Simón said.

Benny bit into the Twinkie just as they reached his block. They parted ways with a series of fist bumps and head nods. But when Benny was a quarter of the way down his block, Ronny called out, "Yo, you live by that boarded-up brownstone, right?"

"Yeah," Benny said. "Why, what's up?"

Ronny just nodded, though. Then he and Simón rounded the next corner, out of sight.

Benny walked down Second Street thinking about Ray and Sylvia and Ronny's headphones and the initials JB. He sat on the stoop in front of his apartment, looked across the street, where Ray lived, and swallowed the last of his Twinkie half. Benny was always answering for Ray. Why was that? And what would happen if Ray messed over Sylvia now? Would Ronny come looking for him, too?

He turned to the condemned brownstone next door. The one Ronny had just mentioned. Tags everywhere, boarded windows, signs warning, Keep Out. He imagined this was what his grandma's lungs would look like if they were an apartment building in Brooklyn. His own lungs hurt just thinking about it. He fell into thinking about her again. What if she got worse? What if one morning she never woke up? And Benny peeked into her room and found her there. No longer breathing.

He looked up when he heard a group of girls from the private school approaching. They stopped talking as they passed Benny and then giggled farther down the street. One girl had on a Santa hat even though it was March. She looked back for a half second and caught Benny's eyes, then continued on with her friends.

Something weird was going down, Benny thought. And it all centered around the mysterious pair of headphones.

Before bed that night, Benny sat with his grandma watching some ancient movie on TCM. He hated old flicks, but his grandma seemed mesmerized by every boring conversation. At least Auntie Rosa had come by with groceries, so there was mint-chip ice cream.

"Hey, Grams," Benny said, setting down his empty bowl.

"Hey what?"

"You know the building next door?"

"Of course I know the building next door, Benny. I've lived here my whole life." She coughed into a closed fist.

"I was just wondering, though," Benny said. "Who owns it?"

She gave a dramatic sigh and made a big production out

of picking up the remote and turning down the volume. "Some silly old Polish lady. Five feet nothing with a hairy mole on her chin. Lives in a trashy studio in Greenpoint with a hundred cats. Refuses to sell the building next door because she hates her ex-husband, who's a racist pill popper. What else you wanna know, huh, Benny?"

Benny chuckled some and looked away. He never knew if his grandma was being serious or playing him. After a few seconds he said, "How much you think it's worth? Like millions?"

"Boy, what do I care?" she said. "None of that money's gonna end up in my bank account."

Benny smiled.

His grandma coughed.

"Okay, let's say you were given all the money in the world, Grams. What's the first thing you'd go buy yourself?"

His grandma stared at his forehead, like she was genuinely thinking about it, which surprised him. "I wouldn't buy nothing," she finally said. "But I might hire detectives to help me find something I lost."

"What'd you lose?" he said, knowing she meant the silver necklace from his grandfather.

She smiled at Benny and patted his knee.

Benny waited for her to answer, but she never did. Eventually she aimed the remote at the TV and turned the volume back up.

Just before three in the morning, Benny awoke from a nightmare.

He flung off his covers and sat up. As he looked into the darkness, pieces of his dream slowly came back to him. . . .

He was in Coney Island with his grandma, where he'd talked her into going on the Ferris wheel. When they made it to the very top, though, she stopped breathing. He screamed for help but the Ferris wheel was stuck. She clutched at her throat, her face turning blue, and all he could do was cry, like some stupid little kid, and beg for his grandma's forgiveness. Because deep down he knew something no one else did. It was his fault. He was the reason his grandma was dying. She'd already raised her own kids. Three of them. But instead of getting to relax in her old age, like most people, she had to watch Benny.

Benny turned on a light and found himself, once again, standing in front of Ray's stupid drawing. He wondered if it was a bad idea to wish something about saving his grandma's life. Since he didn't actually believe in wishes, what if it worked the opposite and his grandma stopped breathing, like in his dream? They'd put him in a foster home. Far away from Brooklyn. And he'd have nobody. Not even illiterate Ray.

Benny decided to wish for something simple first. Like a test. He leaned toward the half-crumpled drawing and said, "I wish for a pizza from Pino's. Not no single slice, either, Mr. Santa. A whole pie, steaming hot out the oven."

His grandmother coughed again in the next room.

Benny shut off his light and climbed back into bed.

First thing he did when the alarm went off was check the stool in the fireplace. He looked around the room, thinking maybe his pizza wish had morphed into something slightly different, the way his first one had gone from earplugs to headphones. But there was nothing.

He shrugged and climbed off his mattress.

When he came back from his shower, he checked again. All around the room. Still nothing close to pizza. He got together his book bag, went to the kitchen, and made his grandma's green tea, put her medicine on a small plate, and set everything on the table in front of her. She was coughing nonstop, though, and didn't even look up at him.

"Hey, Grams," he said, "you all right?"

She waved him away, saying between coughs, "Just go to school, Benny."

He stood there, staring at her. Maybe his dream had been trying to tell him something. That she was getting worse. That she maybe needed an ambulance, and he shouldn't leave her.

He was about to put his bag down and call 911, but right that second she looked up and barked, "Benny. Go to school, I said. Now!"

Sylvia sneaked up on Benny's blind side at the start of lunch period, pinched his side. "So I heard you talked to my bro yesterday," she said.

Julie was a few steps behind, texting somebody on her pink phone.

"For a minute," Benny said. He pulled a textbook from his open locker, slipped it into his bag.

"Yeah, well"—she patted his arm—"whatever you said, he seems cooler about me and Ray."

Benny nodded and shut his locker.

"I'm still thinking of a way to repay you."

"You don't need to repay me," Benny said.

"Nah, I always take care of people who take care of me."

Julie put away her phone and tugged Sylvia's shirtsleeve.

"Come on, Syl. Let's go get Pino's already. I'm starving."

"Okay, okay." Sylvia turned back to Benny, said, "I think Ronny actually trusts you."

"It's his face," Julie said. "Benny's got that kind of face you just believe."

"Maybe," Sylvia said.

Benny felt his believable face going red and he waved them off, said, "I don't know about all that."

"It's true," Julie said, smiling. "I'd trust you." Then she tugged on Sylvia's sleeve again and they both waved and started toward the campus exit.

Benny knew he should have some cool parting line right here, something funny, but he couldn't think. He had to settle for watching Julie walk away.

After school, Ray and Benny stopped by the bodega for candy. Ray paid, which Benny figured was Ray's way of saying thanks without saying thanks.

Outside, the skinny homeless man on the bucket rattled his coins and said the only three words he seemed to know: "Spare some change?"

Ray walked right by, but Benny dropped in a couple more quarters.

As they cruised Seventh Avenue, Ray told him, "You

know that goes right to dude's beer fund, right?"

Benny shrugged. "I also know it's a free country."

They stopped at the corner of Second Street. Ray was going to go play ball, but Benny had to get back to his grandma. Before they parted ways, Ray took another shot at his invention game: "Or what if there was a computer that could do homework, B. Like you'd just stick the assignment in and it'd print out all the work in like ten seconds. Then people could ball and go to the movies with their girl and still pass school."

Benny shook his head, told Ray, "You seriously need to read a book."

Ray waved him off.

"By the way," Benny said, "you know Julie?"

"Yeah, you're digging on her, right?"

"No—I mean, I don't know. I just wondered if you knew her last name."

A smile went on Ray's face. "Bauer. Why, you gonna go stalk her now?"

"Julie Bauer," Benny said. "Her initials are JB."

"Way to go, B. I guess reading books really does make you smart."

Benny decided not to mention the headphones and how "JB" had been etched into the right side. He still thought Ray might have something to do with it.

"Yo, you should wish for a date with her," Ray said. "On the machine I drew you. I can pretty much guarantee it'll come true."

Benny stared at him for a sec. "Wait, what are you talking about?"

"I'm saying," Ray said, "that thing's got magical powers. And Julie's the perfect wish." He started laughing and pointed at his own temple and then turned and jogged off.

Benny's grandma wasn't on the couch when he got home. She was in her room, sleeping. He tiptoed into his own room and found something shocking. A large Pino's pizza box sitting on his cracked stool. He couldn't believe it. He popped open the box, found a mix of slices. Pepperoni and plain and mushroom and garden-style and even his all-time favorite, Hawaiian. They weren't steaming hot out of the oven—in fact, they looked a day old—but that didn't stop his stomach from growling. Plus, his first wish came slightly different from what he said, too.

Benny closed the box without eating any pizza and sat there for a couple minutes, thinking. Nothing like this had ever happened to him. But what exactly was happening? He didn't know.

He got up and opened the closet door, looking for clues. He lifted his mattress. Peeked up into the hollow fireplace.

Opened the window and looked up and down the fire escape. He walked down the hall toward his grandma's room, calling out, "Hey, Grams! You put that pizza in—" He cut himself short when he remembered she was in bed, asleep.

He walked quietly back into his room, remembering how Julie and Sylvia had gone to Pino's for lunch. How Sylvia had promised to pay him back. Then there was Ray bringing up his wish machine picture after school. That grin on his face when he said Benny should wish for a date with Julie. Julie Bauer. JB. Letters that made him think of Ronny's headphones and how Ronny had wanted to confirm that Benny lived by the condemned brownstone. The private school girl in the Santa cap even came to mind. The way she'd turned around and looked at him.

Somebody was playing him.

Benny opened the pizza box again. Looked a little too old to actually eat, though, so he closed it back up.

He imagined if there was a hidden camera somewhere in his room. And people all over the internet were sitting with their bowls of popcorn, watching him. Laughing at him.

Benny spent the next two days trying to make sense of the headphones and pizza. He stopped making wishes because there was a tiny part of him that actually wanted to believe, and the fact that he had even one gullible bone in his body freaked him out.

Still, he'd stare at the ridiculous picture for hours, running through different wish possibilities.

At first he was convinced it was Ray. Who else knew Benny taped his spare key to the bottom of the potted plant on the fire escape out back? Things were heating up with Ray and Sylvia. Ronny had even invited Ray to play pickup with him and his boys. This had to be another example of Ray thanking Benny without actually thanking him.

But on the flip side, how would Ray have known what Benny wished for? It wasn't like he'd planted a microphone somewhere. Benny had scoured his bedroom, the entire apartment. And Ray seemed genuinely clueless when Benny thanked him for the pizza at school. "What pizza?" he'd answered.

"The whole pizza in my room."

"Yo, you got pizza at the house, B? Let's go handle that!"

Even if Ray wasn't directly responsible for the pizza or headphones, he had to have at least told somebody about the spare key.

That led Benny to Sylvia and Julie. They'd gone to Pino's the day he found the pizza in his room. And Sylvia had promised to "repay" him for talking to Ronny. And what about Julie's initials? Wasn't it too much of a coincidence to have those same letters, JB, etched into the headphones sitting on his desk? Maybe they tricked remedial Ray into telling them about the spare key.

Another possibility, though, was Auntie Rosa, who came by with groceries twice a week. She and his grandma hardly talked anymore, and she only stopped by while Benny was at school, but she was consistently inside the apartment. And she'd always liked Benny. Probably because she didn't have kids of her own. Maybe this was her way of saying she'd take Benny in if anything happened with his grandma.

He considered each and every one of these possibilities. But in the end, he always looped back to the same person. His grandma. She was in the house all day. And even though she was tough on Benny to his face, he knew she loved him. This was probably her way of doing something nice for him without getting all mushy about it. Which she hated. At the same time, it worried Benny, too. Because if she was doing something nice, maybe she knew she was coming to the end of her life. Maybe this was her way of saying good-bye.

He tried to put that last part out of his head.

There were still questions. Like how did his grandma hear through the wall? Her outdated hearing aids barely worked when Benny was sitting right next to her. And how'd she pull all this off in a walker? These days it took her like half an hour to even get up the block. There were definitely things that gave Benny pause, but his gut told him it had to be his grandma.

On Thursday night Benny decided to make a special wish.

After he and his grandma watched another boring old movie together, about some big-eared dude trapped on an island during some war, Benny washed up like normal and went to his room and closed the door. He waited until he heard the faint sounds of coughing in the next room, then he positioned himself in front of Ray's wish machine picture.

But instead of leaning toward the drawing this time, he turned toward the wall he shared with his grandma. "Here goes another wish, Mr. Santa," he called out in a louder voice. "I wish for a beautiful silver necklace. To replace the anniversary one my grandma lost from her husband. My grandpa."

Benny put his ear to the wall and listened.

He couldn't hear much, but he could imagine in his

head. His grandma's eyes all bugged as she lay in bed trying to process Benny's latest wish. Which was really her wish.

The next morning Benny's stool was empty. But he was hip to his grandma's game now. A special wish like a silver necklace would need more time.

He showered and fixed his grandma's green tea and set her pills on a plate and put everything on the table in front of her. Then he ate his cereal at the kitchen table, watching her on the couch. She was coughing even more than usual. And she wasn't watching *The Today Show* or reading one of her mystery books. She was just sitting there, staring at nothing.

"You all right, Grams?" he said.

She waved him off and coughed some more.

"Need me to stay home?" he said. "I could take you to the doctor or something."

"You're going to school!" she barked. "Won't be no ignorant kid running around under my roof!"

He finished the rest of his cereal trying to decide if he should stay home to make sure she didn't go searching for the necklace. Because this was the sickest he'd ever seen her. She couldn't even sit up straight. There was no way she'd survive outside alone.

When he went over to her, though, all she did was shoo him out the door.

Benny couldn't concentrate at school.

He listened to his teachers lecture, but nothing stuck. He kept imagining his wheezing grandma walkering herself down Seventh Avenue, coughing nonstop, barely looking before crossing streets.

"You all right?" Ray asked him after history.

"Yeah," Benny said.

"You seem out of it." Ray unwrapped a piece of gum and popped it into his mouth. He offered one to Benny, but Benny shook him off. "Anyways," Ray said. "You know your wish from last night?"

Benny stared at Ray, hoping the next thing he said would clear everything up.

"I'm not supposed to say anything, but it's gonna come true."

"What are you talking about?" Benny said.

"Your wish, B."

Benny was about to press further, but right then Sylvia came up to them and pulled Ray away. They were both giggling like they knew something he didn't.

"What's going on?" Benny called after Ray.

Sylvia was the one who looked back. She made a zipper motion across her lips like neither of them would say a thing.

Benny was sure it was Sylvia and Ray granting his wishes, until Julie caught up with him after school.

"Hey," she said.

"Hey," he said back, hoping she was about to tell him everything.

"Why you in such a hurry?"

"Nah," Benny said. "I just gotta take my grandma to this appointment."

"Oh," she said. "Then I'll just say this real quick. Me and Sylvia were talking last night. And we wanted to know. Or, more like I wanted to know." Julie seemed suddenly nervous as she searched for the right words.

"It's about my wish machine, right?" Benny said, trying to help out.

Julie got a confused look on her face. "What wish machine?"

Benny scanned her face for a grin. "You really don't know?"

"Um, should I?"

Benny stopped walking. "Your initials are JB, right?"

Julie stopped, too. "Yeah. So?"

"Did you put your initials on a pair of Sony headphones?"

"What?" Julie scoffed. "Who puts their initials on head-phones? Besides, I only have the earbuds that came with my iPod."

Benny looked at the ground, more confused than ever.

"Why are you so weird?" Julie said.

"What were you gonna say then?"

Julie shook her head and told him. "I was just gonna see if you wanted to go to the movies on Sunday. With Ray and Sylvia."

"Oh," Benny said. He felt like the biggest idiot in Brooklyn.

"So, do you?"

"Yeah."

"You sure?"

"Totally. I just thought you were saying something else."

She shook her head, told him, "You're really weird, you know that?"

Benny didn't say anything. He knew it was all awkward now, but he was too confused to try and smooth things over.

"Anyways," Julie said. "Sylvia will tell Ray what time, and he can tell you. Now go take care of your grandma. Weirdo."

* * *

As Benny walked home he realized Ray had been talking about Julie earlier. The guy knew nothing about the replacement necklace. Which left his grandma again. Who was too sick to go outside. What if his stupid wish had backfired and put his grandma in danger? He picked up his pace a bit, a terrible feeling growing in the pit of his stomach.

When he got to Second Street he saw two cop cars halfway down his block and his entire body went numb. Then he saw the ambulance. And the fire truck. Lights flashing without sound. The street was blocked off near his apartment.

Benny threw off his book bag and started sprinting.

He tried to run right through the wall of cops standing in front of his gate, but two of them wrapped him up, saying, "Whoa, whoa, whoa!"

"What happened to my grandma?" Benny shouted.

"Slow down, son," one of the cops said.

"What's your name?" another said.

But right then Benny saw the stretcher being wheeled out of his building. He crumbled to his knees, shouting, "No! Please!"

He covered his face with his hands. Looked up at the stretcher again and shouted, "Grandma!"

One of the cops put a hand on Benny's shoulder and

said, "It's gonna be okay, son."

Benny looked up at the man but couldn't see his face. That's when he realized he was crying. And he was on the ground.

"What's your name, son?" another cop said.

"That's my grandma," was all Benny could say back. "That's my grandma."

He wanted to tell them it was all his fault, too. She was too old to have to watch some stupid kid like him. But the words wouldn't form.

The paramedics carried the stretcher carefully down the stairs and then flipped down the wheels and began rolling it out of the gate, toward the waiting ambulance.

Benny wiped his eyes and stood, preparing himself to see his grandma. He prayed she was just sick. Or hurt. Not dead. Not gone forever. Then the stretcher was in front of him and it was his grandma and there was an oxygen mask strapped over her face.

His chest felt like a bottle of shook-up soda. Like any second it would explode right there on the sidewalk. And they'd have to put him on a stretcher, too.

"I'm sorry, Grams!" he shouted.

His grandma moved her eyes to look at him but that was it.

Then she was past him.

"Is she gonna live?" Benny said, turning to the cop.

"Yes, she is," the cop said. "Thanks to that man." He pointed up to the stoop, where a man was being led out of Benny's building in handcuffs. After a few seconds Benny realized who it was. The homeless guy who always sat on a bucket outside the bodega and begged for change.

What was happening? Why was he coming out of Benny's place? And in handcuffs?

The homeless man looked right in Benny's eyes as a female cop moved him toward one of the squad cars. "I only wanted you to believe," he said, and then he lowered his eyes, like he was ashamed.

When they got to the squad car, the female cop guided the homeless man into the backseat and slammed shut the door.

"Did he hurt her?" Benny said, making a move toward the squad car with clenched fists.

But the cop held him back. "You got it wrong, son. That man saved your grandmother's life."

Benny looked at the cop, confused.

The cop motioned toward the condemned building next door, where three firemen were sawing through the padlock on the front grate. "Yes, he broke into your apartment, Benny. But when he found your grandmother passed out on the couch he called nine-one-one on your phone. And paramedics got here immediately."

Benny's eyes went wide as he processed what he was being told. "So why's he being arrested?"

Static sounded over the cop's radio. He held it to his mouth and gave the address of Benny's apartment building and then turned back to Benny and said, "What's your name, son?"

"Benny."

"Okay, Benny. We need to take him in for questioning. We found a gold chain in his possession that we believe was your grandmother's."

That's when it hit Benny.

The wish machine.

The hollow fireplace.

Gold instead of silver, 'cause it was never exactly what he said.

"What's the man's name?" Benny asked.

"Mr. James Burrell. He's already admitted to squatting in the building next door for the past few weeks. We believe he broke into your apartment through a connecting fireplace in one of the bedrooms."

Benny couldn't believe it. He wiped his face on his shirtsleeve and told the officer, "He wasn't stealing the chain, mister. I think he was bringing it to us."

Now it was the cop's turn to look confused.

"My grandma lost her necklace," Benny explained. "Awhile ago. And then last night I wished for it. And he was making my wish come true. Even though it was supposed to be silver like the one she lost. But that's exactly how it was with the earplugs and the pizza, too."

"Pizza?" the cop said. "You're losing me, Benny."

The cop jotted something down in his notebook and then looked at Benny, waiting for more.

But Benny was thinking about something else now. Because he'd made those wishes on Ray's stupid wish machine drawing, the homeless man had come into the apartment and found his grandma and saved her life. All because he had believed. He never would have thought of that.

"Benny?" the cop said.

The firemen were now entering the condemned building, pointing their high-powered flashlights.

The ambulance with his grandma sped away.

Benny took a deep breath, and prepared himself to explain it all, starting with Ray's drawing.

THE DOUBLE EAGLE
HAS LANDED
BY ANTHONY HOROWITZ

There was just one question I had to ask myself. How could I have ended up dangling from a flagpole, twelve stories above a street in North London, with an armed maniac walking toward me, a rabid dog snapping at my fingertips, and the world's worst detective clinging to my ankles? Actually, a second question also came to mind. What was I going to do next?

It had all started earlier that same day . . . a damp, wet Tuesday in January, the sort of day that made you forget that Christmas had ever happened or that spring would ever come. Looking out the window, all I could see was rain. In fact, looking into the window, I could see quite a bit of rain too. The roof was leaking. My big brother, Tim, was sitting behind his desk with water dripping into a bucket beside him. The bucket looked happier than him.

You may have heard of Tim Diamond. He called himself a private detective. That was what it said on his business card . . . at least, it did if you ignored the spelling mistakes. He was twenty-five years old, dark-haired, and good-looking provided you didn't look too closely. Tim had spent three years as a policeman. In all that time he'd never prevented a single crime or arrested a single criminal. The truth was, he wasn't too bright. He once put together an Identikit picture of someone suspected of robbing a bank and the police spent the next six months looking for a bald Nigerian with no nose and three eyes. He did once rescue a woman from drowning but she wasn't too grateful. He'd just pushed her in.

After that he set up his own business with an office in Camden Town. He got the place at a knockdown price, which was hardly surprising as knocking down was all it was good for. There was a reception room and a kitchen, two bedrooms and a bathroom. The pipes gurgled, the floorboards creaked, the windows rattled and the radiators groaned. On a bad day, you had to shout to make yourself heard. He got a sign painted on the front door. It read,

TIM DIAMOND, PRIVATE DETECTIVE, and it looked great, although in my view it might have been more effective on the outside. Still, at least it reminded him who he was every time he left.

To be fair, Tim did get a few cases and you may have read about them in a series of bestselling adventures such as *The Falcon's Malteser, Public Enemy Number Two,* and *South by South East.* Okay—that's an advertisement, but Tim gets 5 percent from the publishers and frankly he needs it. The last time I looked he was down to his last fifty dollars—and we're not even talking American. I'm still not sure what he was doing with a Zimbabwe banknote in his wallet. It wasn't as if he'd ever been there. But that was all he had, and fifty Zimbabwe dollars wouldn't be enough to buy us breakfast . . . unless we went halves on the egg.

And how did I end up living with him? It was a question I'd asked myself a hundred times and I still hadn't got a sensible answer. I'd moved in when I was thirteen, just after my parents immigrated to Australia. I've got nothing against the Australians and their dollars are actually worth the paper they're printed on—but I didn't want to leave London and so I slipped off the plane just before it taxied onto the runway. After that it was a choice between living rough and homeless on the streets—begging off passersby and trying to avoid being arrested and sent to an orphan-age—or moving in with Tim. I'm still not sure I made the right choice.

Anyway, it was my first week back at school and I hadn't had a lot of fun. Either I was growing or my uniform had shrunk in the wash . . . if this went on much longer I'd soon be back in shorts. And of course, I was the only person in the school who hadn't got a new Xbox or a new iPhone or any other expensive gadget with a letter in front of it. Tim wouldn't even have been able to afford a new Tcup, and although Mum and Dad had sent me a card from Sydney (Santa surfing at Bondi Beach), they'd forgotten to enclose the book token or, better still, the check. On the other hand, I knew that things were tight out there. My dad had started a new business selling heated toilet seats but appar-ently the bottom had fallen out of the market.

So I was in a bad mood when I trudged home that Tuesday afternoon. However, as I climbed the stairs, I heard voices and realized that the miracle of Christmas had finally happened, even if it was a few weeks late. Tim had a client!

I let myself in and sure enough, there was my big brother, leaning across his desk with the wobbly half-smile he used when he was trying to look professional. The man sitting opposite him was big and fat. He must have weighed three hundred pounds and my first thought was that I hoped he'd chosen the right chair. He had ginger hair, a round face, and a big smile, although with that hair and that face I wouldn't have thought he had a lot to smile about. He was wearing a crumpled suit and a tie that had only just made it all the way round his neck. There was a scarf draped across his shoulders and leather gloves on his hands. It seemed strange that he hadn't bothered to take them off, even though it was a cold day outside. I guessed he was in his late thirties and if he didn't give up the crisps and the sugary drinks, forty was going to be a stretch. He was smoking a cigarette, which wouldn't help, either. He needed to see a doctor or an undertaker . . . it was just a question of which one would get to him first.

Tim saw me come in. He was obviously in a good mood because he didn't try to throw me out. "This is Mr. Hollywood," he said.

"Underwood," the man corrected him. "My name is Charles Underwood. And who are you?"

"I'm Nick Diamond," I said. I jerked a thumb at Tim. "I'm his brother."

"Mr. Thunderwood needs a private detective," Tim explained. "He was just saying that he needs someone reliable and responsible . . . someone who isn't afraid of danger."

"Then what's he doing here?" I asked.

"I got your brother's name out of the telephone book," Underwood replied. He looked for an ashtray. There wasn't one so he stubbed the cigarette out on the desk. "I have an office in Clerkenwell," he went on. "It's on the twelfth floor of the House of Gold." He waved a hand in the air. "That's what I do for a living, Mr. Diamond."

"What? You're a conductor?"

"No. I buy and sell gold. Mainly old coins. Right now I have a Double Eagle in my safe worth five million pounds."

Tim's mouth dropped. "Your safe is worth five million pounds?"

"No. The Double Eagle is worth five million pounds."

"What? And it's guarding the coins?"

"The Double Eagle *is* the gold coin, Mr. Diamond. It was made in America in 1933 and it's incredibly rare." Underwood leaned forward—as far as his stomach would let him. "It landed in London yesterday . . . it was flown in from Chicago. And now I've had a tip-off that someone is planning to steal it. That's why I need a private detective."

"Why don't you just move the coin?" I asked.

"That was my first thought. But it's too risky. If I walked

out of the office with the coin in my pocket, someone could shoot me or stab me or run me over. . . ."

"They could do all three!" Tim exclaimed.

"That's right. It would be easy to steal it off me. The coin is safer where it is. . . ."

"In the safe," Tim muttered. "But it is a safe safe?"

"It's six inches thick," Underwood replied. "It has a thirty-digit code. The office is locked with a sophisticated alarm system and the building is patrolled day and night. But here's the problem. The man in charge of security—his name is Harry King—he's the man who's planning to rob me. He's going to break in at midnight tonight."

"How do you know?" I asked.

"I'll tell you." Underwood took out another cigarette and rolled it between his fingers. It wasn't easy because he was still wearing the gloves. "First of all, King is a bad sort. I've checked him out. He spent three years in prison."

"He was a guard?" Tim asked.

"No. He was a prisoner. Armed robbery. Of course, you might think he's reformed. I'm all for giving a man a second chance. But the other day I overheard him talking on his mobile phone." Underwood lit the cigarette. Gray smoke curled out of his lips. I was just glad I wasn't one of his lungs. "Even before I found out about his past, I never trusted King," he went on. "He's a sleazy sort of fellow, always short of money. I think he gambles. I hate people who gamble!"

"I bet you do," Tim agreed.

"Anyway, he was standing outside the building with that dog of his—he has an Alsatian—talking on the telephone."

"Wait a minute. Wait a minute," Tim interrupted. "How could the dog talk on the telephone?"

"King was the one talking," Underwood growled, doing a pretty good impersonation of the dog himself. "I heard him say that he'd go in at twelve tonight. He said he would get it and hand it over tomorrow."

"How do you know he was talking about the coin?" I asked.

"I don't. I can't be a hundred percent certain. And that's why I haven't gone to the police. Let's call it a hunch. I just don't think he adds up."

"He's bad at math?" Tim asked.

Underwood ignored him. "I want you to go to the building tonight," he went on. "I can give you a key to the front door. I want you to follow King and see what he gets up to. My office is number twelve-oh-five. If he goes anywhere near it, you call me or you call the police. Tomorrow morning I have a dealer coming to buy the coin.

I just need to be sure it's still there. . . ."

"All right, Mr. Slumberwood," Tim said. "I'll do it. But it's going to cost you seventy pounds."

"I'll pay you twice that to make sure the Eagle is safe!"

"Okay. A hundred and twenty pounds it is."

"I'll give you the money tomorrow." Underwood got to his feet and I almost felt the chair sigh with relief. He slid a plastic entry card onto the desk. "This is an electronic key-card," he said. "It'll get you into the main building. The House of Gold is on St. John Street. You can't miss it."

"Why is that?" Tim asked.

"Well . . . it's got 'House of Gold' written on the front door."

"Good."

"And make sure Harry King doesn't spot you! I don't want him to know we're onto him."

"I'm the invisible man," Tim said. "Everyone who sees me calls me that!"

Underwood was about to leave, but before he went he did something very strange. He picked up the dead butts from the cigarettes he'd smoked and slid them into his top pocket. Why would he do something like that? He didn't look like the sort of man who was interested in keeping the place clean. Of course, Tim hadn't even noticed. He was already imagining the money he was going to be paid the next day. And that worried me too. If Underwood had a five-million-pound coin that he was going to sell, how come he couldn't afford even a five-pound down payment now?

"Tim," I said, once he'd left, "I've got a bad feeling about this."

"Relax, kid!" Tim winked at me. "This case is right up my street."

Yeah. The street to the loony bin, I thought. But I didn't say that. "I'm not so sure I trust this guy Underwood," I went on. "That story he told you . . . the security guard talking about the robbery on his phone. Don't you think that's a bit unlikely?"

"Not really. Lots of security guards have phones."

"I mean, talking about a robbery when he can be overheard! Also, Underwood didn't pay you. And he told you to ring him if anything happened, but he didn't give you a number!"

"Look, Nick," Tim interrupted. "It's a simple job. All I have to do is follow the security guard and see what he gets up to."

"Okay," I said. I knew I was going to regret this but I felt I had no choice. "But I'm going too."

"Where are you going to?" Tim asked.

"I'm coming with you, Tim."

"Forget it, Nick. No way. Absolutely not. No chance."

"So when do we leave?" I asked.

Tim nodded. "As soon as it's dark."

The House of Gold might have had a fancy name but it was just an ordinary office building in an ordinary street. It was twelve stories high with a flagpole sticking out below the roof, and as I glanced up at it for the first time, I never thought that in about half an hour, I was going to be clinging to it with both hands with Tim clinging to me by both ankles. But maybe that's my problem. I just don't have enough imagination.

We let ourselves in using Underwood's card and, to be honest, part of me was surprised that it even activated the doors. I'd thought it was going to be as fake as him. We found ourselves in a reception area with half a dozen potted plants that looked half-dead and wilting . . . which was quite surprising as they were actually made of plastic. There was an empty reception desk and on the wall a list of names. More than fifty jewelers and gold dealers worked at the House of Gold and there was the name, Underwood, with the number—1205—among them. That surprised me too. Charles Underwood hadn't looked like a coin dealer to me. Everything about him had smelled wrong . . . even his aftershave.

There was no sign of Harry King or his dog but that was just as well. I had no desire to get arrested or bitten . . . and who knows? If he'd seen us, Harry might have done both.

Tim was wearing black jeans, a black jersey, and a black balaclava covering his face. Frankly, he looked more like a burglar than a private detective and more like an Alpine skier than either. I was still wearing my school clothes. Tim had a flashlight but he didn't need it because there were lights on throughout the building. Anyway, the batteries were dead, and it occurred to me that any minute now we could be too. I had a nasty feeling about this. Half of me wished we hadn't come and the other half agreed.

"There's a lift!" Tim waved his flashlight in the direction of a corridor leading away from the reception area.

"Forget it, Tim," I said. "We can't risk it."

"What? You think it might break down?"

"No. But somebody might notice it moving. Let's take the stairs."

We found the staircase and began the long climb up. There were sixteen steps between each floor and twelve floors. I counted every one of them. Finally, we got to the top and found ourselves in front of a pair of solid-looking swing doors that met in the middle with metal plates and wires positioned so that they connected. It was like the entrance to a vault or to a top secret laboratory or something. I stopped to catch my breath. Perhaps we should have taken the lift after all.

"Tim . . . ," I began.

"What?"

"I'm not sure you should open these doors."

"Why not?"

Tim pushed them open. At once about a hundred bells all around the building began a deafening clang. A recorded voice burst out of hidden speakers shouting "Intruder Alert! Intruder Alert!" Somewhere, a dog started howling. Searchlights positioned in the street exploded into life, blasting the windows, blinding us. In the far distance, about fifty police cars turned on their sirens, shattering the still of the night as they began to close in.

"Do you think the doors are alarmed?" Tim asked.

I grabbed hold of him and began to drag him back down the stairs. All I knew was that this was the sophisticated alarm system that Underwood had mentioned and we had to get out fast. If the police arrived, how were we going to persuade them that we weren't actually trying to rob the place ourselves? But I'd only taken two steps before I realized that the howling was coming from below me and about half a second later, the biggest dog I had ever seen turned the corner and began to bound toward us.

By big, I mean big . . . perhaps a hundred pounds of knotted muscle and fur. Its eyes were ablaze and the last time I'd seen so many teeth I was looking at a crocodile. The dog was leaping toward us with a look in its eyes that simply said "dinner"—and it was clear that Tim and I were the ones on the menu. Behind it, I glimpsed a uniformed figure who I guessed must be Harry King. He was black and bald with arms and shoulders you could use to advertise a gym. Frankly, I've seen friendlier sumo wrestlers. He was about ten steps behind the dog. They were both heading our way.

"This way, Tim!" I shouted.

We burst through the double doors. It was too late to do any more damage. The alarms were still jangling and the recorded voice was louder than ever. "Intruder Alert!" I think we'd got the message. The police cars were getting nearer too. It was like the whole building was under attack. I was already wishing I'd stayed at home. I'd left behind two hours of French homework—but even that would have been more fun than this.

We found ourselves in a long, dark corridor with offices on both sides. One of them had to be 1205 but I didn't stop to check the numbers. I was thinking of the dog coming for us. The doors had swung shut behind us and that might hold it up for a moment. But a moment wasn't long enough. What was I looking for? A second staircase. A lift. A fire escape. A helicopter launchpad with a helicopter just about to take off. Anything to get us out of here.

"In here!" Tim had found a door and burst through it. I didn't bother following him. With typical brilliance, he had found his way into the gents' toilet. I waited for him to come out again and at that moment the double doors swung open and the dog came pounding through. Tim was holding something and hurled it in the dog's direction, and at least that distracted it for a few seconds. In the meantime, I found another door. This one opened onto a staircase that climbed up. We took it. We had nowhere else to go.

The staircase led to a door that took us onto the roof and before we knew what had happened we were out beneath the stars with a freezing January breeze whistling around us, reminding us we'd be much warmer inside. Unfortunately, Fido was also inside, and given a choice between catching a slight cold and being ripped to pieces,

I knew which I preferred. Without even stopping to catch breath, we set off across the roof. Surely there had to be another way down.

Then two things happened at once. The dog burst through the same door that we'd just taken. That was when I realized it was rabid. White foam was pouring out of its mouth, and its eyes were bulging and discolored. At the same time, Harry King appeared. I wasn't sure where he had come from but he was suddenly there, making his way toward us, and he was holding something in his hand. He raised it, pointing it in our direction.

"It's a gun!" Tim shouted.

To be fair to him, he was trying to protect me. I mention this only because it was Tim who nearly killed me. Thinking that Harry was about to fire, he rugby-tackled me to the ground. The only trouble was that there was no ground. At that moment, we were right on the edge of the building, and with a certain sense of surprise I realized that, in his attempt to protect me, my big brother had just thrown me into thin air with a twelve-story fall and a concrete pavement waiting for me below. I was also aware that Tim was coming with me. I don't quite know why, but part of me was glad that we were going to be together at the very end. This seemed an unusually stupid way to die, even by

Tim's standards. I'd have hated to do it on my own.

But we didn't die. You've probably guessed what happened next. I saw the flagpole and managed to grab hold of it, and at the same time, Tim managed to grab hold of me. And that's how this all started (you can go back to the beginning if you've forgotten) with the two of us dangling in the air like a couple of comedians in those old black-and-white movies except without the honky-tonk piano and the laughing audience.

I don't think I'd have been able to hold on for more than about thirty seconds. My hands felt like they were being pulled off my wrists. My feet felt like they were being pulled off my ankles. My shoulder blades and spine weren't doing too well, either. Looking down, I could just make out my big brother, swaying in the breeze. And looking up . . . ?

Well, suddenly Harry King was there, leaning over the edge. The dog was with him. But neither of them was trying to kill us.

"Hold on!" Harry shouted. He lay on his stomach and reached down with one hand and I felt his fingers close around my wrist. I could tell at once that he was incredibly strong. It was like being seized by a crane. And then, inch by inch, he was pulling me up—and Tim with me. My fingers found a grip on the edge of the building and I was able to help him, pulling myself over the top. At the same time, Harry got a stronger grip under my arms. He was panting with the effort. The dog—still foaming at the mouth—was wagging its tail. This was all very strange. We weren't being chased anymore. We were being saved.

I felt solid ground underneath my chest, then my thighs as I was pulled onto the roof. Tim came with me. As soon as I was safe, Harry reached past and helped him up the rest of the way. Down below, I could hear the police cars pulling in. There was the thud of car doors and feet hitting the pavement. Somehow I knew that the ordeal was almost over. But I still didn't quite know what it was all about.

"Are you okay?" Harry demanded. Looking at him close-up, I could see that he was a friendly, pleasant sort of man. But then, he had just saved my life, which may have helped change my opinion. He certainly wasn't carrying a gun. What Tim had seen was actually a walkie-talkie . . . and it made my head spin to think that this had been enough for him to throw both of us over the edge of a twelve-story building.

"Thanks," I muttered.

"Who are you? What are you doing here?"

I didn't answer. Too much had happened too quickly.

Then the first police made it up onto the roof and I was almost grateful when we were both placed under arrest.

There's not a great deal more to tell.

I suppose I should start with the man who had come to the office and who had told us his name was Charles Underwood. It wasn't. The real Charles Underwood visited us in our cell and he turned out to be silver-haired, about five foot three, and Irish. He wasn't very happy, either. Because while Harry King had been chasing us, while the police had rushed up to the roof and arrested us, someone had slipped into his office and stolen his precious Double Eagle coin.

I only had to explain it all to Tim five or six times before he understood. The fake Underwood was the thief. Somehow he'd got a key to the building—which he'd given to us—but he hadn't been able to get past the security system in order to crack the safe. So he'd used us as a diversion. We'd been spotted by CCTV cameras the moment we entered—that was how the police had got there so quickly. We'd set off the alarms. We'd been chased onto the roof. And while everyone was busy dealing with us, he'd had ample time to open the safe and make off with the contents.

And while I'm tying up the loose ends, I might as well mention that Harry King had never been in prison, and his dog, Lucy, didn't have rabies. When Tim had ducked into the men's toilet, he had picked up a bar of soap and that was what he had thrown as we ran for the stairs. The dog had eaten the soap—which was why it was foaming at the mouth.

They never did find the thief. Of course, we gave the police a description, but the man who had come to our office could have been wearing a wig. He could have had padding under his jacket. He must have heard about Tim from somewhere because it can't just have been luck that had made him choose the most stupid detective in London. Tim had played right into his hands. And of course those hands were wrapped in gloves, so although the police searched our office, they didn't find so much as a fingerprint. Our visitor had been careful to take his cigarette butts with him too—making sure he left no DNA.

He was one of the ones who got away but that's what happens now and then. In fact, where Tim Diamond is concerned, it happens quite a lot of the time. A happy ending? Well—I hadn't been killed. I hadn't fallen twelve stories and fractured every bone in my body. I hadn't been chewed up by the dog. And speaking personally, I was perfectly happy with that.

PIRATE

BY WALTER DEAN MYERS

My name is Abdullah Syed Hari. My great-grandfather was born in a gleaming white house just southeast of Marka. He was a fisherman who had worked those waters for all of his life. My grandfather, too, was a fisherman. His black hands were hard and the fingers twisted from years of pulling the nets into the boats, mending them in bad weather, and so full of salt that he could not feel my face except by turning his hands so that the backs would touch my cheek. My father's gift was music and he played in the evenings after coming home from a day on the sea and the songs soothed me when I was a child. In the wars before I was born, clan against clan, friend against friend as Somalia tore itself apart, he was wounded and made cripple. I am

Abdullah Syed Hari. I am a Muslim, the very servant of God. I am fourteen years of age. And I am a pirate.

My father tells me that when the first foreign boats came, our fishermen didn't think much of them. But soon we saw that what they could do was far more than what we could do. We had boats and they had ships with huge nets that caught five times as many fish as our boats could even carry. Sometimes their steel ships would push our boats from the best fishing grounds.

"Their fishing boats could eat ours," my friend Kambui said, "and still be hungry."

This was certainly how it seemed to me. They came from Norway and Germany and Japan and from all the countries of the world beyond Somalia.

Other ships came, too. Sometimes they would drop barrels into the water, barrels mostly sealed, but some of them leaked a fluid that turned the water dark. Some of the fish off the shore began to die. They would float onto the beach, their bodies white and shining under the hot sun, until the tide left them to rot and for the gulls to eat.

Then the gulls began to die.

Obe Bashir Hari, my uncle, said that what we must do was plain for all the world to see.

"We have to fight back or watch our families starve," he

said. "They want to pretend that they don't see us, but we must insist upon being seen." This was what he said to my cousin and my father when he first became a pirate. When my father asked if I would go with them, my uncle looked at me and felt my arm.

"Yes," he said. "The boy is old enough to fight. He should go."

"They are polluting our lives," my father explained to my mother. "They are making even our dreams dirty."

My mother looked at me sadly and nodded. She had often spoken about how many boys from Marka had already gone.

"They have to take you young people to do the killing and the dying," she said. "The rest of us are already too tired of it all."

The evening that we left she put her hand on my arm and told me to walk with God. But even as she spoke she looked away.

Mussa Cali is nineteen years old and he is our leader. He is very black in color and also speaks well. He first went to war when he was sixteen and the enemy was the peacekeepers with their blue United Nations peacekeeper helmets. They had tried to stop the people from raiding the government food stores. The peacekeepers were beaten back but he had sustained a scar across his forehead that seemed to move when he was angry. Then he had teamed up with the Volunteers, who provided weapons when they were needed by anyone who attacked the foreigners. They also took part of whatever was taken. Mussa sometimes talks about how the foreigners have no business in our waters, but I know he is a pirate because he likes the money he gets. He has bought a motorbike for himself and for his uncle, who tears around the city like a madman.

This was my second trip. The first trip we got nothing because an American navy boat came up on us as we neared our target and we had to turn away.

Our boat, six meters long with two nearly new engines, was called *Raqq al-Habib*, after a song the owner liked. If we were successful we would paint it over and change the name before going out again. Our families came to the beach with us and kissed us many times before leaving. Then the guns were handed out and packages of cooked rice and spicy lamb. When I was handed a gun, my heart pounded in my chest. I told myself to look calm and I tried to think calm thoughts, but I knew I was close to shaking, I was so afraid. The men kissed Mussa on both cheeks and embraced us all.

"It's good to see young warriors." A man with a small stubble of a beard touched my head.

The *Habib* was a very special boat. It had a false tiller mounted on the back that had no real use and a wheel in the cabin. My uncle said that the tiller made it look like a slow boat but the twin screws would let it fly across the water.

I had a band of ammunition that was slung across one shoulder and that came down past my waist to my hip. My uncle showed me how to release the safety of the AK-47.

"You will know who the enemy is and where to point the gun when the time comes," he said. His voice was higher than it was in the marketplace or when he sang at home. It was high and wavered and I knew that somewhere inside of him there was also fear.

I said a small prayer to God and told him that I did not want to die, knowing that if he could read my heart he already understood this. There were seven of us altogether, and I imagined seven prayers drifting to heaven.

Mussa let the boat drift without turning on the engines, watching the water lap along its sides, letting the strength of the tide rock us gently. It would be a weak tide, someone said. A weak tide on a dark night.

When satisfied that he knew the tide, Mussa turned on one of the engines. The *Habib* started off toward the middle of the gulf.

When I was young I used to sit by the old piers, sometimes on one of the pilings they used to moor large boats, and dream of a time when strangers came to Somalia in boats with huge masts and gleaming white sails cutting across the blue sky. My mother, with a smile in her voice, called me a dreamer.

"Everyone under cover except Abdullah," Mussa said when we had reached a point where the tide was most affected by the opening to the gulf. I watched as the others crowded into the small cabin.

Mussa turned out the light and let the boat drift. I peered into the darkness but saw nothing except shadows that could have been only in my mind. Then, in a moment when the clouds parted and allowed rays of the dim moon to shine through the fog, I saw our target.

The yacht was twice as big as our boat, with a high cabin just ahead of the boat's center. It was moving slowly through the fog and darkness, its wake barely troubling the water. I looked at my watch. Nearly midnight. The sidelights swept over us as it sounded a warning blast of its horn.

"It's coming toward us, Mussa!" I called to him.

"Sh!" Mussa worked the false tiller to make it look like he was trying to turn away.

The fog was thin and I could see the sleek white boat slow and turn. There was a rail around the wheelhouse.

Brriiing! Brriiing! Its alarm sounded again. I looked at Mussa as he turned toward the yacht and shrugged his shoulders.

Brriiing! Brriiing!

The alarm sounded again and I could see someone in the wheelhouse moving. The yacht veered sharply to its right and I could hear the engine of the *Habib* rev up for a second, putting us at an angle as the two boats drew closer together.

"Watch it, you fool!" shouted a voice from the yacht. Our two boats were touching!

"Sorry!" Mussa cried. "Very sorry!"

The moment he said that, the first two men sprang from our cabin, crossing the small deck quickly and leaping up to the deck of the yacht. The next two followed immediately, screaming as they jumped onto the boat.

The white gleam of the yacht's body was like a ghost as it lurched toward us. The sound of our machine gun sent a chill through me as our fifth man stood and shot just toward the radio mast. I looked toward Mussa and he signaled me to be still.

On the yacht there were nothing but shadows darting here and there. The shouts were sharp, almost like barking dogs. Mussa was on his toes straining to see what was happening. The man with the machine gun shot short bursts from his gun.

A long minute passed. And then silence.

"Completed!" Ahmed, a young man who fancied himself a good footballer, appeared at the rail with his forearm around the neck of a short white man.

We tied our boat to the yacht and we all climbed aboard it.

There were six people on the yacht, which was about fifteen meters long. As Ahmed pushed them down into the rear well of the boat, Mussa shined his light in each face. The first was the white man that Ahmed had brought to the rail. He was small and fat and his eyes rolled wildly as he tried to understand what was happening to him. Mussa had plastic ties, and spun the man around and bound his hands behind his back. Then he kicked his legs and forced him to the ground.

The next white person pushed to the deck was a woman, younger than the man and harder looking. When Mussa tried to turn her around, she spit on him.

Smack!

The blow stunned her. Her eyes widened and her mouth flew open.

Smack!

Now everything was gone from her and she sank to the ground. Mussa twisted her arms behind her and fastened them roughly. I heard her cry out but it was only for a moment and then she was still, bent forward, her face down. I looked away.

The next was a dark man with curly hair; he had been at the wheel and I thought he might be a Yemeni.

"What are you doing?" he called out.

Mussa hit him across the face and I saw that the blow left a smear of blood that came from under his nose and across his cheek.

The next person brought on deck was a girl. She was pale white, her blond hair falling down about her shoulders. Her whole body trembled as Mussa pushed her against the side wall.

Another older man was brought up and a young man who I thought probably worked on the boat as a helper.

Mussa sat on a bench and started going through some of the papers he had found. He went through the small stack, then turned them over and went through them again.

"What do you do for a living?" he asked one of the men. "Tell me quickly before I kill you."

"I'm a news producer," the man said. "I'm very sympathetic to you people."

My uncle was already on his two-way radio talking to the Volunteers who had organized the raid. He told them that things had "worked out well" and that all was in order. My uncle spoke Somali, but the voice replied in Arabic to arrange the hostages quickly.

Mussa heard also and ordered the people from the yacht taken to separate rooms so they couldn't speak to each other. The two men who I thought worked on the boat were taken to the engine room. The producer was taken to the galley. My uncle told me to follow him and took me and the girl to one of the cabins.

"Shoot her if she tries to escape," he said in English. "Or if you hear any shooting anywhere on the boat, then shoot her, too."

I saw her eyes widen and knew she was frightened. My uncle closed the door and she turned and looked at me, and then away.

The yacht was so beautiful. It was grander than my home or the home of anyone I knew. The wooden furniture was polished and gleamed in the soft light of the lamps. In the cabin I was in with the girl there was a narrow bed, a desk with books and pens, two cups, and a small statue of an elephant with its trunk up. I imagined the people sitting in the room smoking American cigarettes and having tea as they sailed. It was a life that was hard to imagine myself being in.

I knew what would happen next. Mussa would report everything to the Volunteers and they would decide what to do next. Maybe we would get into our boat and leave with whatever things of value we had found, or maybe we would hold the people for ransom. If we did that, we would be exposed on the water and it would be very dangerous. I felt my mouth go very dry. There was water in the cabin but I didn't want to drink in front of the girl, to let her know that I was afraid.

From the rhythm of the rocking boat I knew the tide was changing. A long time before, when I first went to sea with my father, he would say that each changing tide was another chance to do well. I hoped that we would do well, that we would not have to shoot anybody. Mussa meant what he said about shooting people, but I also remembered what my grandfather said one night sitting by a fire.

"Human blood is heavy, and slows the feet of he who has shed it."

I have never shot anyone, or fired a gun in anger.

The bed looked perfect, the way they do in movies, and I wondered what it would be like to curl up on it and fall asleep. Would my dreams be different? Would I feel more alive when I woke up?

"Do you speak English?"

The girl's voice startled me.

"Yes," I said.

"Are you going to kill us?" she asked.

"Maybe," I said. It was unkind but I was more interested in myself than in the girl. I did not want her to die, but more than that I did not want to have her blood on my hands.

If we did kill these people, I knew all the boys in the village would ask me to tell them about it. They imagine taking a boat to be exciting and a happy thing to do. I did, too, until my uncle gave me the gun.

"My name is Erica," she said. "I'm twelve."

"I don't care about your name," I answered her.

She began to cry and I knew she thought we were going to harm her.

I hoped we would take what the whites had and leave as quickly as possible. Mussa would take the money and whatever else we found to the Volunteers, who would give us Somali shillings in return and make sure our passage back home was safe. If the Volunteers thought the whites were important enough for us to hold for ransom then it would be very dangerous, for someone might try to rescue them.

Two weeks earlier the Somalian accounts of the raid on a French boat said that French commandos had attacked aggressively, but that one of the hostages had been killed.

"The French have already killed one of the hostages," they said on the radio. "They will think many times before doing that again because it was not very popular in Paris."

But they did not mention the two men from our village who were also killed.

"I have to pee," the girl said.

"I don't care," I said.

"Please!" She leaned forward, hunched her shoulders and crossed her thighs.

I didn't want to call my uncle or Mussa because it would have looked as if I couldn't make a decision. I went to where she sat on the deck and quickly moved her body around so that she was facing away from me. Then, putting my hands under her shoulders, I lifted her to her feet.

"What is your name?" she asked.

"Shut up!" I opened the door to the small bathroom in the cabin. There was a toilet and a sink. I had never had a toilet in my house. It was gleaming white.

I pushed her in and closed the door.

"You have to take my pants down!" She pushed the door open with her foot.

She was shorter than me by about two inches. Her gray eyes looked up at me and she still moved as if she had to pee very soon. "Turn around," I said.

She turned and I took off the plastic cuffs. "If you try to get away I will shoot you," I said.

I didn't close the door completely but sat away from it, keeping my automatic trained on the framed rectangle. There was a design on the door that matched the statue on the desk. I listened to hear sounds of her peeing, trying to remember her name. It didn't come to me but then I thought of what would happen if we were captured. Would she say that I had let her pee? Would she remember my face?

Suddenly the door to the cabin opened and Mussa came in. He looked around quickly.

"Where is the girl?" he demanded.

"She had to use the bathroom," I answered.

He quickly opened the door and I saw her sitting there, both hands in front of her. Mussa reached in and grabbed what she had in her hand. A cell phone. She was texting a message to someone!

He jerked her out by the hair and sent her sprawling across the floor.

"Were you sitting on your ears? You didn't hear me say to watch her?" he was shouting at me. "You have killed us, you idiot!"

Two steps was all he needed to cross the small cabin.

For a wild moment I thought he was going to shoot the girl. Then I saw him draw back his rifle, holding it like a cricket bat, and start a swing. I turned and looked toward the girl but it was my face that received the blow. The pain shot through me and for a moment my senses reeled in an explosion of colors and confusion.

I was on the deck in so much pain it wasn't bearable. It was all I could do not to cry out but I thought he might hit me again or even shoot me. My left eye didn't open but with my right eye I saw that he was turning the girl over and was putting the plastic cuffs on her again. On the floor against the wall was her telephone.

Mussa was still yelling. I couldn't distinguish what he was saying, but in a moment the door opened and my uncle came into the cabin.

"This fool let the girl make a phone call!" Mussa said, pointing the AK-47 at me. "Now we are dead. If the army is notified, we can't go back to shore unless the Volunteers make a deal. No deal, and we will be shot like dogs right here on the water."

My uncle looked down at me, and then he kicked me in the stomach. I knew he had to do that. The mistake was mine and I had to pay for it. Maybe later, if we all lived through this, they would decide to kill me anyway. My uncle had to show his displeasure.

Mussa took my weapon from me and put it next to the girl with the muzzle against her neck. Then he put my hand on the gun.

"If she moves, kill her, fool," he said. "And if you don't, I will kill you!"

Before he left, my uncle looked down at me, at the fool I was, and spit on the floor.

I felt so bad. All the things I had wanted to make better, the empty nets that made empty bellies, the dead fish floating on the incoming tide, the children getting sick from the water in the wells—I had thrown away because I wanted to let a white girl pee. In my heart I was crying because I knew I had let my people down.

The porthole was open and outside I could hear the sounds of seabirds screeching and the cool rush of the early morning breeze. I knew that the Volunteers had immediately been told what I had done and were cursing me. Without doubt the girl had told someone that the yacht had been taken, and the army had been notified. They would cover the shore and shoot us if we approached so that they would look good on the morning news. Now we had to keep the prisoners and bargain with whatever country or company they were from in hope that they would give us money in return for their lives, or that, at the very least, they would let us live if we did not kill them.

"I'm sorry," the girl said.

I looked at her and she was crying. I opened my mouth to say something but nothing came out. My left eye was still throbbing with pain. It felt swollen and my hand was trembling as I raised it. I didn't mind the pain. I wanted to hurt and to feel sorry for myself. It was me, Abdullah, the servant of God, that had brought us to this situation. If the helicopters came and their snipers killed me, I wanted to at least suffer for my sin.

"What is your name?" she asked.

"Abdullah," I said.

"I'm sorry, Abdullah."

What did she see? Did she see me bleeding and pitiful, my one eye closed, looking at her like a pitiful dog?

The boat rocked and I thought I was going to vomit. Thoughts came but nothing clearly. I remembered seeing television images from when the French retook a sailing yacht that my people had captured awhile ago. On European television they showed the French commandos, dressed in their uniforms, storming the ship. But on our television they showed the first Somalis when they were hit by sniper fire. No one had known that the French were not going to negotiate. No one until the first bullets hit.

Minutes passed, then hours. I was relieved for ten minutes and the girl was allowed to go to the bathroom, but the door was left open so she could be watched. Afterward she sat again on the floor with her hands bound behind her.

"What do you think will happen?" she asked when we were alone.

"Maybe we will die," I said. "I don't know."

Crying. She was crying again. If I could have been braver I would have put my arm around her and told her that I didn't think we would die. It wasn't what I believed but only what I hoped.

A noise! *Ch-ch-ch-ch-ch-ch-ch!* A helicopter.

"Abdullah!" My uncle opened the door roughly. "Go up to the deck. Leave your hands by your side. Don't touch your weapon, but let them see it. Now! Quickly!"

My legs were weak. Stumbling, I made my way up the six steps to the well deck.

The helicopter was above us. I looked up and saw the big gun protruding from the side and a soldier with a rocket launcher pointed down at me. There was no one on the deck except me.

"Hold your hands out so they can see them!" Mussa's voice came from the darkness.

Ch-ch-ch-ch-ch-ch-ch! The helicopter made a slow circle

in the air. I looked down and saw the red target beams crossing my chest. One crossed my face. At any moment I could be killed.

A single shot hit the deck next to me, splintering the wood. My teeth couldn't be still in my mouth. The helicopter moved again, more red target beams crossed my body, and then the huge, deadly bird moved away into the darkness.

"They didn't kill him," Mussa said. "They're still thinking!"

The night passed slowly and as the first gray rays of morning entered the cabin I thanked God for giving me another day. The girl Erica was asleep, lying on her side. I was nearly asleep when I heard footsteps. It was my uncle.

"The Volunteers have worked out a deal," he said. "We leave the hostages aboard except for one man, who we will turn over to the army. The Volunteers will get two hundred fifty thousand dollars. From that the Volunteers will keep half and the army will get a quarter and we will get a quarter.

"It's not a bad deal unless they have made another deal that we don't know about."

"What will happen if they have made another deal?" I asked.

"They will kill us as we pull away from the yacht," my

uncle said. "It depends on how much they want to save these people."

When it was time for me to leave the girl, I freed her wrists. She rubbed her hands together and looked up at me.

"I'm sorry that you were hurt," she said, touching my hand. "I thought I was doing the right thing."

"I don't know if there is a right thing that fits everybody," I said.

We had lived. When we reached the shore there were a few soldiers waiting for us but many more Volunteers, all with weapons beneath their coats, or nearby in case the soldiers tried to betray us. Some of the people cheered us and that was good. Mussa came over to me and said that all was forgiven.

"We finished with a profit," he said. "We have done well, little brother."

It was what I expected from Mussa. When we get the money we will be generous with it and my mother will talk to me again about going to London or Brussels or anyplace away from Somalia. But I won't leave.

In Marka when the sun is high the people don't cast large shadows because they are thin. It is just a small shadow, almost as if it had been casually cast upon the hard ground. Old people laugh at the shadows of thin people, but they can laugh because we are not farmers, but fishermen. When the sun is too hot and the ground is too hard to grow what we need to survive, and when the fish die, their white bellies facing the sun as they float onto the shore, it is a different world than the old people know. It is a different world than the white girl, Erica, knows. I think of her going to school and telling her classmates about being captured. I wonder if she will remember me as a fool or as somebody who just wanted to let her pee? I wonder if she will ever look at a map of Somalia and think about what is happening here?

I will never know. Each of us will live in the memory of the other for a little while, but we will fade away. That is the human way, I think.

THAD, THE GHOST, AND ME

BY MARGARET PETERSON HADDIX

The ghost boy is trying to talk to me.

"Please," he moans in his wispy voice. "Please help me."

I ball my hand into a fist and punch him in the stomach.

"See," I say over my shoulder to my cousin Thad. "It's not real. It's just one of those fake hologram things they always have at haunted houses. See how the ghost goes away when I block the light?"

The thing is, even though he's pale and see-through and barely even there, the ghost doesn't go away. I move over to the right, then back to the left, and no matter what I do, the ghost boy's image stays whole.

Whoa, I think. *How'd the Bloomingburg Bunnies and*

Chicks 4-H Club get their hands on such smoking hologram equipment?

I picked the wimpiest-sounding haunted house in three counties to take my cousin Thad to. Me, I like them all, the scarier the better. But Thad—don't get me wrong. He's a good kid. He'd have to be, being related to me and all. But he's just a little bit . . . disadvantaged.

Yeah, that's the right word for it. He's had to put up with stuff like his parents thinking it was cool to name him Thaddeus Eugene. And calling him that in front of other people. And making him take violin lessons instead of playing football like me. And telling him it might be dangerous to build a potato cannon or shoot a marshmallow gun. (I mean, marshmallows! Really? Really?)

All that wasn't so bad when he was just a little guy. People always think little kids with big round glasses are cute. But Thad's in fifth grade now. I have exactly ten months to get him ready for middle school.

If I don't, those middle school kids are going to eat Thad alive.

I should know. I just started middle school this year.

So even though it kind of creeps me out that the ghost boy isn't going away—and, in fact, seems to have really felt my punch and is doubled over in pain—I don't let on. I look back at Thad, who's pressed his scrawny body so tight against the opposite wall that he could almost be part of the ugly flowered wallpaper. Maybe he's going for a camo effect with the haunted-house graffiti painted over the ugly flowers: KEEP OUT! and DIE! DIE! DIE!

I smile encouragingly at Thad, anyway.

"We're really lucky," I tell him.

"W-w-w-why?" Thad asks. "B-b-because the flesh-eating zombies who hang out with ghosts haven't found us yet?"

For a moment I wonder how Thad knows about flesh-eating zombies. Oh, yeah—I told him. Somebody had to. Aunt Myrna almost never lets him watch TV, and he's not allowed to read anything scarier than *Heartwarming Dog Stories*. He's never even seen a PG movie. Sick, huh? Disadvantaged, just like I was saying.

The ghost in front of me lifts both arms, trying to grab my shoulders. Of course his hands go right through me, but I have to stop myself from taking a step back. This really isn't a good time to think or talk about flesh-eating zombies.

"No, I mean, we're lucky we got here before the crowds," I tell Thad—staying focused, just like my football coach is always telling me to do. "We have the place to ourselves."

"Except for the g-g-ghost," Thad stammers.

"Yeah, here's the thing," I say. I turn around completely, turning my back on the ghost so I can look Thad square in the eye. "In middle school, you're going to have to be brave enough to face a lot worse things than fake ghosts. So we're going to start small and build up. Fake ghosts now, maybe one of those killer sled ramps over Christmas break—we keep at it, you'll be the bravest sixth grader at Morrow Middle School by next August."

"And I'll be okay even if I get Hatchetface Hutchinson for English class?" Thad squeaks. "Even if I have a run-in with one of those big kids who already shave? Like Anthony Gorgonzola?"

I have to hold back a shiver at the mention of Hatchetface Hutchinson—who is actually my English teacher—and Anthony Gorgonzola who, so far, doesn't even know I exist. I'd really like to keep it that way. But just hearing those names sets off a flood of frightening images in my brain: Hatchetface Hutchinson breathing down my neck, scolding in her cackly voice, "Now, where should that comma go?" and acting like she'll give me the death penalty if I answer wrong. Anthony Gorgonzola strutting around like he owns the school—I've seen the principal hide from him, like even she's afraid to stop him when he sneaks across the parking lot to hang out with the high school kids at lunch.

And did I mention that Principal Van Sutter herself is a pretty scary-looking woman?

"Right," I say. My voice comes out sounding almost as wimpy as Thad's. I shake my head to push the horrible images from my mind. I resist the urge to turn around to see what the ghost is doing behind me. I clear my throat and regain my focus.

"Now, here's the plan," I tell Thad. I sound strong again. Confident. "You're not going to be able to count on me being around all the time next year in middle school. You've got to get brave enough to be okay even when you're alone. So I'm going to walk on through the rest of the haunted house, all the way to the end, and you're going to stay in here with this ghost for . . ."

I was going to say "fifteen minutes," but I just can't, not while there's so much panic spreading across Thad's face.

"Five minutes," I say, and even that feels like I've just done something awful, like kicking a kitten.

"No, please," Thad whimpers, and his voice sounds like it did when he was a toddler. You shouldn't ever have to be this mean to someone you used to drive around in a Little Tikes Cozy Coupe when you were three.

It's for his own good, I remind myself.

I turn toward the doorway and hurry out, before I can go all soft and change my mind. Out of the corner of my eye, I get a glimpse of the ghost, who's floating over toward Thad now.

"Will you help me?" the ghost asks him.

Keep walking, I tell myself. *Keep. Walking.*

I wonder if my parents felt this awful when they dropped me off at day care for the first time, or sent me off to kindergarten or—did they even know what I was getting into?—watched me get on the bus for middle school. Didn't they see Anthony Gorgonzola lurking at the back of that bus? Didn't they ever have a teacher as terrifying as Hatchetface Hutchinson?

You can still hear Thad if he screams for help, I remind myself.

I'm hoping the rest of the house will be scary enough to distract me from worrying about Thad, but it's just dusty and deserted. There's a bunch of old-fashioned toy soldiers on the floor in the dining room. And there's a petrified-looking loaf of bread on the kitchen counter. Except for a little more graffiti—including words you wouldn't think 4-H members would be allowed to use—that's pretty much it. No more ghosts pop out at me, no one chases me with a chainless chain saw, no one even asks me to stick my hand in a bowl of cold spaghetti to pretend it's brains or guts.

Guess the Bloomingburg Bunnies and Chicks 4-H Club blew their whole haunted-house budget on spray paint and that one sweet hologram projector, I think as I let myself out the back door. And they're not going to make their money back because nobody's here but me and Thad.

I sit down on the back step, which is just an old, decaying wood plank balanced on concrete blocks. Above my head, the same kind of fake-official signs hang on the back door that Thad and I saw at the front: CONDEMNED: THIS STRUCTURE AT 458 GNARLED PINE DRIVE IS SCHEDULED TO BE TORN DOWN ON OCTOBER 31 and NO TRESPASSING: VIOLATORS WILL BE PROSECUTED TO THE FULL EXTENT OF THE LAW.

I've got to admit, the signs are a nice touch. Authentic-looking. Just like the ghost. But still—why wasn't there any fake blood? Or a strobe-lit murder scene? Or volunteers dressed up like vampires and zombies and ghouls, all jumping out at Thad and me at once?

For the first time it hits me just how weird it is that, if you don't count the fake ghost, I haven't seen a single other person since we got here. I was so focused on training Thad to be brave that I didn't think about the fact that nobody was at the front door taking our money. We just tossed it into a box on a table in the front room and kept going.

You'd think a 4-H club would have a bunch of people standing around offering to sell you home-grown pumpkins or something when you got done. And, really, it's the weekend before Halloween. Why don't they have any other customers?

I didn't exactly tell Aunt Myrna we were going to a haunted house. I said we were going to the church hayride—which we are! We are! Just not until later tonight. So she dropped us off at the Methodist church five blocks away, and then Thad and I walked to the address I printed out from the internet.

I dig in the back pocket of my jeans and pull out the folded-up printout: HAUNTED HOUSE, it says, 548 GNARLED PINE DRIVE. . . .

Suddenly I have chills.

Five forty-eight? I think. *Five forty-eight? I thought for sure it was 458!*

I look back at the sign on the door. Then I peer across several backyards toward the next block. There are dozens of cars lining the cross street, with people getting in and out. And beyond that street, on a back porch that's much bigger than the rotting piece of wood under my rear, there's a whole crowd of people laughing and talking and joke-screaming. They look like they've just come out of a haunted house.

A fake haunted house, I mean, the kind that a 4-H club puts on as a fund-raiser, just for fun.

Not like the one I'm at, one that's old and empty and—

Real?

I jump up and race back into the house. I don't think about my own safety. I don't think about my own fear. I'm more focused than I've ever been before in my entire life.

"Thad!" I scream. "Thad! Get out of there!"

I race past the petrified bread on the kitchen counter and the toy soldiers on the dining room floor. I step on one of them and it crunches under my foot and I don't even break my stride.

I burst into the room with the ghost, and he and Thad are sitting together in matching velvet chairs.

"Thad!" I scream. "The ghost is real! This house really is haunted! Run!"

I kind of expect Thad to jump up and start screaming like a maniac—well, like I'm screaming—but he doesn't move.

"Thad!" I shout again. "Are you too scared to run?

Do you need me to carry you? Didn't you hear me? The! Ghost! Is! Real!"

Now Thad moves, but only a little. All he does is clutch the arm of his velvet chair a little more tightly.

"I knew that," he says.

"But I told you it was fake!" My voice goes all high and squeaky. I'm kind of running around in little circles in front of Thad and the ghost, because I'm too scared to stand still. But I pause for a second. "Did you think I was lying?"

"Just for my own good," Thad says patiently. "I thought that was part of teaching me to be brave. Kind of like how Dumbo learns to fly thinking he has a magic feather, until he builds up his confidence, and then—"

"Don't talk about Disney movies!" I snap.

"Oh, right, because then people will think I'm a baby," Thad says, nodding to show he remembers what I've told him before.

"No, because sometimes it's a time to talk and sometimes it's a time to run, and this"—I grab Thad's arm and start pulling—"this is a time to run!"

I've been pushing and pulling and shoving Thad around pretty much since he was born, and he always just goes along with it. But he picks this moment to go all independent on me. He digs his fingernails into the velvet chair arms and locks his leg and arm muscles in place.

And—he's stronger than I thought. I can't get him to budge.

"We can't run away now," Thad says. "It wouldn't be fair to Harvey."

Harvey?

I look over, and the ghost boy is pointing to himself.

"Harvey Herkimer Baldridge," he says, bowing slightly. "At your service."

It figures the ghost boy would have an even worse name than Thad.

"We owe him," Thad said. "We trespassed in his home."

"Oh, you mean all those 'No trespassing' and 'Condemned' signs on the doors are real, too?" I ask. "Not just . . . decorations?"

I glance over at the ghost boy again—Harvey—and his face looks like he wants to say, "No, duh." But the words that come out of his see-through mouth are, "Much as it saddens me, that is indeed the truth of the matter."

Okay, I'm still scared out of my mind, but I can't help but think, *Hatchetface Hutchinson would love to hear this guy talk.*

I remind myself to focus.

"Okay, okay," I say quickly. I force myself to stand right in front of Harvey. I kind of bow myself—there's just something about seeing a kid in a frilly shirt and suspenders and knee pants like his that makes you think you have to bow. And then I say as fast as I can, "I'm-really-sorry-about-the-trespassing. It-was-an-accident. Sorry-for-punching-you-too. I-didn't-know-you-were-real. My-bad. Mucho-apologies."

The last part is the best I can do after just two months of learning Spanish at school. I'm hoping I said it fast enough that Harvey will think it's Latin. Hatchetface Hutchinson says people are always impressed if you use Latin.

"Now let's run," I tell Thad.

"No," he says, shaking his head stubbornly. "Harvey told me his story. He needs our help. I want to help him."

And then I'm stuck. Half of me still wants to run. The other half knows I could never leave Thad behind like that, in danger.

"And," Thad says, "there's a treasure. . . ."

We're in the ghost boy's basement now. I'm a little fuzzy about what time period Harvey's from—it's hard to remember to ask smart follow-up questions like, "You say your father died in the war. Which war?" when your brain is still screaming, *Run! Run! Why aren't you listening to me and running?* But Harvey's family definitely lived here before anybody figured out that "basement" was supposed to be a code word for "place with giant flat-screen TV, wall-to-wall carpeting, and ginormous cozy recliners and couches for watching sports."

Harvey calls this place a root cellar. He told us to climb in through the coal chute because some "intruders" boarded over the regular doors after Harvey's family left.

Huh, I wonder why. Who wouldn't want constant access to a swampy mud pit that smells like someone died down here?

Oh, no! Oh, no! What if Harvey died here? What if he wants to kill us here on the same spot, to avenge his own murder?

This thought kicks up the volume of my brain's constant *Run! Run! Get out of here!* so loud that my ears stop working for a moment. But how can I run when Thad's just standing there smiling up at Harvey? It's not like it's a competition, but . . . what if it turns out that Thad is actually braver than me?

Harvey is about halfway through with floating down through the basement ceiling. He told us he couldn't climb down the coal chute because he can't leave the house. It's so freaky to see him hovering up by the ceiling. Right now I can see his legs dangling from the bottom of a rafter. Now it looks like that rafter decapitated him. Now it looks like he's hanging. . . .

Think about something else! I tell myself. *Ordinary stuff. There's plumbing pipe down here. You know about plumbing pipe, because that's what you built your potato cannon out of. And everyone thought you were so cool. And you are. And, see, this is really just like any basement, except for the muddy floor. And that safe over there. Who keeps a safe in their basement?*

It's a giant black old-fashioned-looking box, almost as tall as Thad. The safe has four number dials on the front that could be the great-grandfather versions of the one on my locker at school.

Studying the safe calms me down, too.

Harvey has floated all the way down to the floor by now, and I'm able to keep my voice steady to ask, "So, is the treasure in the safe?"

"I admire your powers of deduction," Harvey says, and he sounds so polite I can't tell if he's making fun of me or not.

It would be great to have that skill in middle school.

"Harvey told me all about this upstairs," Thad says.

"See, he knows the combination, but his hands always go right through the dials—"

"And would go right through the treasure if I tried to pick it up," Harvey adds. He demonstrates by swiping his hand through the safe.

That part of being a ghost would kind of stink.

"So you tell us the combination, and we'll turn the dials for you," Thad says, sounding a little too eager.

"You do it," I say. "It will be good practice for next year at middle school when you have a locker."

Harvey gives me a look, and I almost think he can tell how much trouble I had with my own locker, that first week of school. I really was planning to train Thad on combination locks. Once I, you know, had enough practice myself.

Harvey tells Thad the numbers, and Thad sets each dial carefully. The lock clicks and the door creaks open.

Like a crypt, I think. A tomb. Maybe Harvey just tricked us into letting out all the flesh-eating zombies?

For a moment, I'm wishing I'd never seen anything but G-rated movies, and never played any video games after Reader Rabbit. I can picture about ten billion different kinds of monsters that might come swarming out of that so-called safe in the next few seconds.

But nothing happens except that the door stops when it's separated from the rest of the safe by only a crack. Thad grabs it and yanks it the rest of the way open.

And there, on the floor of that giant safe, lies . . .

A single sheet of paper.

"That's it?" I say in disappointment. "That's the huge, giganto treasure that you've been haunting this house for?"

"Yes," Harvey says. You wouldn't think it was possible, him being a ghost and all, but he's grinning like crazy. The whole time since I met him, I've mostly been trying not to look at him. But now I do. And—he kind of looks like he would have been a fun kid to hang out with, when he was alive. It looks like he had freckles and red hair and a cool gap between his front teeth that he could probably whistle through.

When he was alive.

Thad reaches into the safe and pulls out the paper, and all three of us huddle together to look at it. I see lots of made-up-sounding words like "whereas" and "heretofore."

"What is it?" Thad asks.

"It's my brother's will," Harvey says. "Written long after I died. He wanted to leave this house to the side of the family who would take care of it. Not the miscreants who let it fall into such shameful disrepair."

"Yeah, well, no offense, but why isn't your brother the

one haunting people, trying to get them to find his will?" I ask. "Why'd he send you to do his dirty work?"

I'm not sure I really want to know all the ins and outs of ghosts and hauntings. But I am kind of curious.

"Because my brother died in his sleep as a ninety-year-old man at Willow Knoll Nursing Home," Harvey says. "I died here, in this house. Protecting this house."

I take a step back.

I knew it, I think dizzily. *Next he's going to point out his half-buried skeleton in the corner of the dirt floor. . . .*

I bang my elbow against one of the plumbing pipes, and it knocks the seal loose. The pipe falls to the floor.

Harvey gives me a cold look. Hey, it's not my fault his brother hid his will too well and let the house go to, uh, miscreants.

"Don't worry," Harvey said. "I didn't die down here. I fell from the roof when I was eleven and three-quarters years old. I was repairing the roof after a huge storm. I was the man of the house after my father died—I was doing a man's job—I was almost done. . . ."

He puffs out his chest a little, like he's really proud of himself. But then he seems to remember that it killed him, and he slumps again.

"We must right this wrong," he says, sweeping his arm in a ghostly way that trails vapor toward the sagging pipes, the rotting rafters, and maybe even all the way to the CON-DEMNED signs out on the house's doors.

I don't want to become a ghost anytime soon, but it would be sweet to be able to do that.

"What do you want us to do for you now?" Thad asks, all eager beaver all over again.

See, that's just the kind of thing that's going to get Thad killed in middle school.

I flash Thad a "down, boy" look, and puff out my chest just a little. I say to Harvey, "Whoa, there. Hold on. Me and Thad said we'd help you find your treasure. We didn't make any promises about righting any wrongs."

I'm trying to think how to explain, without sounding like a chicken, that righting wrongs sounds dangerous. Like, we might have to deal with the people doing the wrongs.

Harvey gives me a look that, I swear, is just like the one Hatchetface Hutchinson gives my class when someone says something really dumb.

"The only thing you have to do," Harvey says stiffly, "is place my brother's will in an envelope and mail it to the county courthouse. That will take only a penny or two. And I believe the postal service makes its rounds twice a day, so you can select the time that is most convenient for you."

I'm about to tell Harvey, "Oh, come on. Stamps never cost just a penny. Did they?" or maybe, "Since when does the mail come twice a day?" Or maybe I could really shock him by saying, "Let's just use email. It's free."

But just then we hear a bunch of loud noises overhead: enough thumps and thuds for an entire convention of ghosts and ghouls and maybe even flesh-eating zombies.

"Um," Thad says nervously. "Why didn't you tell us that you have other, uh, friends, haunting this house with you?"

And it's written all over his face that he's thinking, *If those are more ghosts, please let them be friendly. Whatever they are, please let them be friendly. Please, please, please* . . .

"Those aren't ghosts," Harvey says, and it really bothers me that he looks nearly as terrified as Thad. "I fear—" He stops, as if whatever he's afraid of is too awful to put into words. He grits his teeth—probably the same way he did climbing onto the roof before he died—and he says, "I will go up and see for myself. You two stay here."

Like he thinks we're going to follow him?

Harvey shoots up through the rafters. A second later he's back, moaning.

"It's them!" he cries. "My worst fears are realized!"

And now he's really freaking me out, shooting around the room in a panic. I am so proud of myself that I can stay all calm and cool and collected and manage to croak out, "Uh, who? Who is it?"

Harvey settles back down to the floor beside Thad and me, but he still flickers nervously back and forth.

"A group—no, a gang—of troublemaker boys," he says. "Older than us. Since the last tenants moved out, these boys have come here a lot. They swear and curse and everything."

He sounds as horrified as my grandmother. I'm thinking that Harvey had better never hang out in the eighth-grade wing of my middle school. The shock would kill him, if he wasn't already dead.

But all this calms me down.

"Enh, what's the worst thing they could do?" I ask, shrugging.

"They write on the walls," Thad says. "They—"

He breaks off, because it sounds like the entire gang of troublemaker boys has trooped into the room right over our heads. They are stomping and shouting, and I can hear someone calling out, "That's right—let's burn it down now. The whole house is going to be torn down next week—we'll just help things along!"

And the next sound we hear—is that a match being struck?

I wouldn't have thought it was possible for a ghost to

turn pale, but Harvey does. He looks like he could faint.

Me, I just freeze.

Two boys found burned to death in basement of abandoned house, I think. What if me trying to make Thad brave just gets both of us killed? What if we get stuck haunting this old house—or what's left of it after it burns down—for the rest of eternity?

But Thad—he's actually grinning.

"Harvey," he says. "You're a ghost! Scare them away!"

Oh, yeah. Why didn't I think of that?

But Harvey's already shaking his head.

"Believe me, I've tried," he says. "They can't see or hear me. Only certain people can. Otherwise, don't you think I would have gotten help finding the will before now?"

I take a deep breath.

"Harvey, could you go back upstairs and see if they've started the fire yet?" I ask, in my best trying-to-stay-calm-when-I'm-really-terrified voice. "So we know how much time we have to—"

The word exploding in my mind is "escape." But Thad jumps in and says, "Right. We need time to plan how to stop them."

Is he nuts?

Without saying a word, Harvey zooms back up through the rafters to check out the action above us. While he's away, Thad says excitedly, "I bet it's only the pure-hearted who can see ghosts. That's why we can and those bad kids can't."

I'm trying to figure out how to say, "And why would being able to see ghosts be a good thing? Why do you act like it's a reward?" But Harvey is already back, looking slightly less worried.

"No flame has yet been set to the walls of my beloved edifice," he says, which I guess means they haven't set the house on fire yet. "They're arguing about whether they should have a new troublemaker do it, a dark-haired fellow I haven't seen before—they say he has to go through some sort of initiation first. There are five of them, and they're all talking at once, and no one's listening, so that should give us—"

"Enough time," Thad says, and even though I've known him all my life, it's like he's suddenly turned into some-body else. His eyes are shining behind his glasses, and he chops at the air with his hands, like a general giving out orders. "They're older and probably bigger, and there are more of them, so we're going to have to use the element of surprise." He reaches back and grabs the plumbing pipe I knocked away from the wall a few minutes ago. He holds it out to me. "You can make a potato cannon with this

I pause to aim, two things hit me.

One: Did Harvey say, "kill someone"?

Two: Is that Anthony Gorgonzola, the scariest-looking kid in eighth grade, in the center of the gang? Pinned down—like the rest of the gang is even meaner than him?

I want to stop everything. I want to run away. I want to throw up.

But Thad has already shot his petrified bread at the gang, and I can't leave him without backup. I close my eyes and blow as hard as I can into the end of the plumber's pipe.

Ping!

The toy soldier I aimed hits a wall right over the gang's heads. Without pausing to think, I'm reloading, shooting again. And so's Thad.

Ping! Ping! Ping!

Neither of us can aim very well, but he manages to clip one gang member's ear, and I hit one in the back. And we have surprised them. In the split-second flashes of looking up before I reload and fire again, I see the gang jumping up, screaming, "Bullets! We're under attack!" and "We're surrounded!"

Maybe these guys were brave enough to give themselves tattoos. But they're terrified of a few lengths of plumbing pipe, some bread crumbs, and a handful of toy soldiers.

In the flickering light from the candle, I see the gang take off running out of the house. I hear the front door slam behind them again and again: *Bang! Bang! Bang! Bang!*

Only, they're in such a hurry to get away that someone drops the candle.

"The carpet!" Harvey cries, floating over the hungrily licking flame. "It's on fire!"

Thad and I rush forward, stamping out the flame. Thad snatches up a flashlight that one of the gang members dropped, and he's swinging the beam around the room as if that's a way to look for more flames.

Someone grabs my ankle.

"I think you just saved my life," a deep voice says.

Thad swings the beam of the flashlight toward the voice, and my heart practically stops.

It's Anthony Gorgonzola, the scariest eighth grader ever, still lying on the carpet.

Why didn't you count how many times the door slammed? my brain screams at me. *Why didn't you worry more about your own life than Harvey's carpet? Why . . .* My brain hiccups a little, overwhelmed.

"Wait a minute," I say to Anthony Gorgonzola. My voice

shakes only a little. "What did you just say?"

Before he has a chance to answer, the front door creaks open yet again. The whole room is bathed in one of those bright spotlights that police use at crime scenes. And, running out of the light, is yet another of my nightmares: my English teacher. Hatchetface Hutchinson.

But she totally ignores Thad and me—and Harvey—and rushes over to hug Anthony Gorgonzola.

"My son!" she cries. "I knew this was too dangerous!"

"Stop it, Mom," Anthony says, pushing her away. "I had to risk a little danger to get the evidence to convict those losers." He pulls out a wire from under his shirt—clearly some sort of recording device. "And I did. It's all right here. They listed every single one of their crimes during the initiation ceremony."

My brain is still stuck on an earlier part of the conversation.

"You two," I say, pointing from Anthony to Hatchetface Hutchinson and back again. "You're related?" I gulp. "Why doesn't everybody know that at school?"

"That would have made it really hard for me to work undercover," Anthony chuckles, and he doesn't sound like the toughest kid in eighth grade anymore.

"My son works for the sheriff's office," Hatchetface

Hutchinson says. "My coworkers and I tipped him off to a crime wave at our school. A gang of older boys has been recruiting middle schoolers to commit certain crimes for them, because the younger kids get lighter sentences if they're caught. . . . It's just lucky that my Anthony has such a baby face that he could still pass for a fourteen-year-old, to get the evidence he needed."

I decide not to tell her that I wasn't completely fooled. Or that I saw the principal letting Anthony sneak over to the high school.

"Yeah, but these kids saved the whole project—and me," Anthony says, pointing at me and Thad. "The gang figured out I was an impostor when I kept stalling about setting the fire. They were just pulling out a knife. . . ."

I hide a shiver. I am really glad I never saw that knife.

But then Hatchetface Hutchinson narrows her eyes at Thad and me, and it's like her gaze alone is as fearsome as any weapon.

"And what were the two of you doing here?" she asks.

I am so relieved that Thad steps forward. In his innocent, little-kid voice, he says, "We were on our way to the church hayride, and we heard someone calling for help. I guess we scared off the bad guys. And we put out the fire. And we found this paper lying around. Do you think it's something important?"

He holds out the will, and Anthony and his mom peer at it. Even Hatchetface Hutchinson doesn't look the least bit suspicious of Thad's story. And—it's not really even a lie.

I guess he's going to do just fine in middle school next year.

Hatchetface Hutchinson starts gasping.

"Millie Van Sutter's family has been looking for this document for years!" she said. "Now she will inherit this house, and she will stop the condemnation proceedings, and she will be able to fix it up. . . ."

"Um, would that be the same Millie Van Sutter who's the principal of Morrow Middle School?" I ask.

"Of course," Hatchetface Hutchinson says.

I flash a triumphant look at Thad, to make sure he gets it. This is good for both of us—we really are going to survive middle school. The principal is going to have our backs.

But Hatchetface Hutchinson is looking straight at me again.

"You're in my third-period class, aren't you?" she asks. "Currently struggling just to keep a seventy-eight-percent average?"

I decide to take a page out of Harvey's book, and say

what the ghost said to me way back at the beginning of this whole adventure.

"Much as it saddens me," I admit, "that is indeed the truth of the matter."

Hatchetface Hutchinson raises an eyebrow.

"Ah, but I am confident that your grades will improve," she says.

"You're going to give me better grades because I saved your son's life?" I ask.

"No. You're going to earn them, because now I know you can," she says.

Okay, that could have gone a little better. But—it also could have gone worse.

A bunch of police and sheriff types swarm into the house. I can see more law enforcement officers arriving, and four heads being shoved into police cars out in the street. I look around for Harvey to see how he's taking all these new developments. He's got to be falling all over himself, ready to thank us for saving his house and scaring off the gang and making sure Principal Van Sutter inherits the house like she's supposed to.

But Harvey is nowhere in sight.

I dig my elbow into Thad's side.

"Where'd Harvey go?" I whisper. Nobody else hears me

because the law enforcement types are busy talking to each other and Anthony and Hatchetface Hutchinson.

"Harvey's right there," Thad whispers back, pointing at blank space. "Can't you see him? Jumping up and down and shouting, 'Thank you! Thank you! *Gratias vobis ago!*'?"

No way Thad could be making that up. I think that last part might even be Latin, and he wouldn't know anything about that.

I swallow hard.

"I can't see him anymore," I admit. "Do you think that means I—I—"

I can't even say it. It's not like I wanted to be whatever that sappy term was that Thad came up with—pure-hearted? Was that it? But still . . . where did I go wrong? What did I do that was so bad when I was trying so hard to be brave and protect Thad and help Harvey?

"Oh!" Thad says, like he's surprised. "Harvey just explained what happened. He says no one can see him once they get older than he was when he died. So you must have just turned more than eleven and three-quarters."

I think about this—yep, my birthday was nine months ago. It makes sense. I'm kind of sad, because I was thinking it might be fun to keep hanging out with Harvey after tonight. But I'm kind of proud, too. I'm the oldest kid here.

(Anthony Gorgonzola definitely doesn't count.) I outlived Harvey. Now that I know I'm going to survive middle school, I'm pretty sure I've got a great life ahead of me.

"Oh, yeah," Thad says, whispering to the air. Then he turns to me. "Harvey says he just heard one of the cops say this whole story is going to be on the front page of the newspaper tomorrow. With our pictures." He clutches my arm. "Mom's going to find out we didn't go straight to that hayride."

I don't even flinch.

"You know, Thad," I say. "Tonight we survived a ghost, a gang, and Anthony Gorgonzola and Hatchetface Hutchinson. Don't you think we can handle Aunt Myrna?"

Thad relaxes. He grins at me.

"You're right," he says. "No sweat."

Wonder if there's a way to say that in Latin?

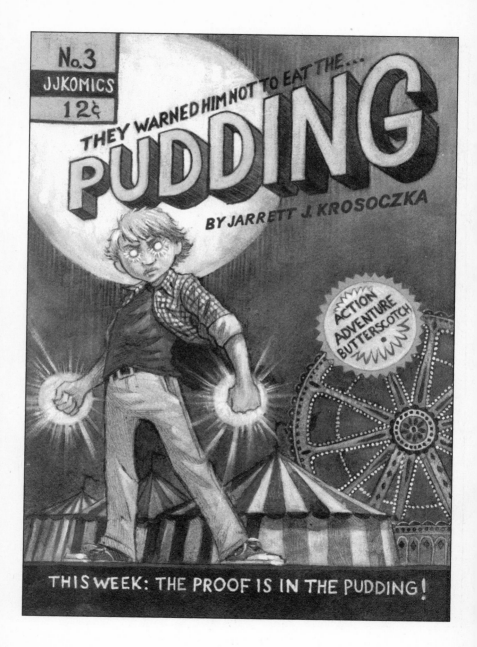

144

THE SNAKE MAFIA
BY GENNIFER CHOLDENKO

In my dream, it was a tiny snake, green—the color of new leaves—no thicker around than a thumb and glowing iridescent like it was lit from within. Slithering so assuredly, it was almost as if it could walk on its coils. It slipped from chair to chair until it reached the door.

No one saw it but me.

It is hot and hot and hot in the blistering heat of the valley, where just walking across the pavement makes your feet burn like dough in frying fat, and the dust covers everything in a dull brown film.

I pour a quart bottle of water over my head, which makes me feel better for the three or four seconds it takes to empty, but by second five the sun sucks the water right off me like a giant drier in the big hot sky.

I'm headed for Homework Club to pick up my little brother, Niko, who is right this second standing on top of the play structure. Oh man, I hope he doesn't jump again. I don't feel like spending the rest of the day in the emergency room. Niko has broken his arm twice, fractured his tibia, sprained both ankles, and lost three teeth. Kind of amazing given the kid is only seven. I think the Red Cross has him on their danger-watch list. *Ripley's Believe It or Not!* is probably interested too. He takes after my dad. My dad is an investigative journalist. He asks the questions people don't want to answer. We see him on TV, when someone's slamming the door in his face.

I'm cautious like my mom. She used to keep my dad and Niko in check. Now that's my job. It's not fun being the cautious one, that's for sure.

On Tuesdays and Thursdays my dad teaches a journalism class at the university, so I pick up Niko. Only me, my dad, and our neighbor Harpreet are allowed to check him out. Harpreet lives next to us. He's tall, wears a white turban, and has the kind of sweet brown face that makes you wish he was your uncle. He's a graduate student and he drives a taxi, which he treats like a slightly irritating relative. When he's driving, he keeps up a nonstop conversation with the car under his breath. In English when the taxi is behaving. In Hindi when it's not.

But today Harpreet has a class so I'm picking up Niko.

Niko is very civilized until we're out of sight of Homework Club, and then he pounces on me, pounding me with his fists, until I pin him to make him stop. Today he does this without his usual vigor since it's one hundred and thirteen degrees in the shade. He pops open his water bottle and pours it over his head, puffing up his cheeks, jumping across the boiling-hot pavement.

We are both half Japanese, but Niko's half is larger. People sometimes come up to him and start speaking in Japanese, which never happens to me.

Niko has the kind of sturdy body that looks like it belongs on the ground, which makes his penchant for jumping even more surprising. I am longer and leaner, but my feet never leave the ground.

We're almost home when we see the black Mercedes careening down the street, over the curb, crunching the gravel planter and nicking the saguaro in front of the Desert Sun. The car is out of place on our street, which is full of apartments for college students and people who teach part-time, like my dad. When it passes us, Niko goes motionless as if he's receiving satellite signals. "River, that was Dad," he says.

"It couldn't be. He's at work. Besides, we don't know anyone with a Mercedes."

He sucks his bottom lip, thinking about this.

I pull my cell out of my pocket and hit the Dad icon just as we turn the corner to our apartment—one of four in the complex. My cell rings through to Dad's, but a beat later, I hear his jazz ringtone in the distance. Uh-oh. He must have forgotten his cell.

It's Niko who notices our apartment door is wide open. He gets in before I do.

"River." His voice is small, pushed down like it's coming from the toe of his shoe.

The coffee table is flipped on its back. The file cabinet from my dad's office is pulled into the living room. The photos on the walls are knocked every which way.

The room Niko and I share has not been touched. My dad's bedroom looks fine, too. It's his office that was torn apart, his desk chair shoved over, his bookshelves pulled from the wall. Computer gone. Printer upside down. Books and papers overflowing into the living room. Even the pencil sharpener is pulled apart—pencil shavings scattered across the floor.

I'm trying to take this all in and think clearly what to do.

I know my dad would say, if everyone is safe, then whatever the problem is we can work it out.

I'm safe. Niko is safe. But what about Dad?

In the kitchen there is a smaller mess. One chair tipped over, a McDonald's bag on the table, and a half-finished Coke. My dad doesn't eat fast food so it isn't his. The Coke is still cold—the ice isn't even melted yet. Whoever did this must have just left.

I'm about to call Dad at work when I see Niko behind me. He's busy putting a pig in a blanket in the microwave, which he does every day after school.

"River." Niko's voice is torqued.

My heart starts hammering. What if the kidnappers are still here? No, I would have seen them. When I turn to Niko, he's focused on the pig in a blanket box. He shoves it in my face.

A note is scrawled on the top in my dad's writing, only wobblier, like he was writing with the wrong hand.

HARPREET IS TAKING YOU TO SCHOOL TOMORROW. DON'T CALL THE POLICE. DAD.

"Don't call the police? We have to call the police," I say.

The microwave dings. Niko pulls out a pig in a blanket

and takes a bite. After the nuclear holocaust, pigs in a blanket will still be here, and Niko will still be eating them.

"Nu-uh. Call Dad," Niko mumbles, his mouth full.

I try to call him, but it's an automated phone loop—a never-ending Möbius strip. There's no way to get a live person. The best I can do is leave a message.

We slog into the mess in his office searching for his laptop. Doesn't look like it's here, but that doesn't mean he has it. Maybe *they* have it. Whoever *they* are.

I checked out a laptop from school, so I get on it and email Dad.

Emergency! Our apartment was trashed. Come home.

"Harpreet?" Niko suggests between bites.

"He's got class. He won't answer until he gets out, which is at six, I think." I wish Harpreet wasn't quite so conscientious. I wish he'd check his texts in class just this once. "Are you sure Dad was in that car?"

Niko nods. I text Harpreet anyway.

Call us!! Emrgncy!

Then I pick up Dad's phone and begin nosing around his call history. Harpreet, pizza man, vacuum repair, the university, Aunt Julie, Snakeworld, Critterland, U.S. Fish and Wildlife Service.

My dad doesn't like to talk about what he's working on,

but it doesn't take honor roll to figure out it has something to do with animals.

"Why would he tell us not to go to the police?" I mutter.

"Maybe he's in trouble with the police," Niko offers.

"Dad?" I snort. Dad likes danger but not the lawbreaking kind. He's a fanatic about following the rules. He considers putting the recycling in the wrong container a felony offense.

Maybe Dad really wants us to go to the police, but the people who nabbed him forced him to write that note. I'd think that was a stronger possibility if he hadn't written on Niko's pigs in a blanket box. A real kidnapper wouldn't write a note on biscuit-wrapped hot dogs. Besides, only Dad would know Niko would find it there.

If we go to the police it will make the kidnappers mad. I don't even know if they're kidnappers though. Dad isn't a kid. Besides, they didn't ask for money, not that we have much, but still. Maybe we're not supposed to go to the police because the police here are corrupt. Are the police here corrupt? I have no idea.

I check a news site my dad works for. His last byline was six weeks ago for a story about endangered species. I don't think Australian monkey-faced bats are going to be ransacking our house, eating Big Macs, and writing notes on hot dogs. I'm betting it's not what he's already written, it's what he's about to reveal.

"Niko, do you know what Dad's been working on?"

Niko keeps chewing. "Snakes," he says.

"Snakes? Dad hates snakes."

Niko shrugs.

Niko has a point, though. Dad has been talking a lot about snakes. I don't much like snakes either. In fact, I had a really creepy dream about a snake just last night.

I look again at the call history on Dad's phone. He left two texts today. *Gd luck. You'll ace Wrld His*, he texted me this morning. And, *Meet me at Marie Callender's Orange and Rte 80*, he texted to a phone number I don't recognize. That text was sent three hours ago, but it doesn't say when they'd meet. Whoever he was texting must have already known that.

"Niko," I tell him. "We gotta find Dad."

Niko has a death grip on his pigs in a blanket. He's not about to go anywhere. "What about Harpreet?"

"We'll be back by the time he gets home. We're only going to Marie Callender's."

Niko checks how many are left. I snatch the box out of his hands, put it in a plastic bag with handles, and give it back to him.

"How will I warm them up?" he asks.

"In this heat, you can cook them on the pavement," I tell him.

He appears to consider this as I chuck my cell on the counter in favor of Dad's—which is nicer—grab money from the emergency envelope in the junk drawer, and water bottles from the freezer.

I head for the utility room to get our bikes, dragging Niko with me.

Outside the air is hot as a furnace, but I don't care. I jump on my bike and pedal as hard as I can down Fifty-first and up the hill to Orange with Niko not far behind. When we get to the restaurant, we ditch our bikes in the gravel and head for the front door. I'm just thinking I should have brought the bike locks when out of the corner of my eye I see our car.

"Niko!" I point toward the old red Subaru parked under a jacaranda.

"Daddy's here." Niko's voice squeaks with hope.

We head straight for the restaurant. He has to be inside. When I pull open the Marie Callendar's door, I'm hit by a wall of air that cools my sweaty face. We run through the restaurant, searching the booths, the back tables, the counter, the men's room. Niko even checks the kitchen, but no Dad.

We walk slower now, not sure where else to look. "Can

I help you?" a hostess with drawn-on eyebrows and a smell like scented candles wants to know.

"Did you see a tall man with dark hair and a beard?" I ask her.

"I don't think so," she says, wiping her hands on her skirt, "but it's been pretty busy today."

"His car is here," Niko insists, crossing his short arms.

She nods. "He'll probably be right back then. Do you want a table?"

"No," we tell her, and head back out to the car, then walk all the way around it, inspecting it like a birthday gift. It isn't locked—"nothing in here to steal," Dad always says.

Inside the car is an inferno, all the compressed heat of the afternoon jammed into one space. The back has our beach towels and bathing suits from last night, when Dad took us to the university pool, an old copy of *Captain Underpants*, and an empty can of tennis balls.

The car is so old you operate the windows with a crank. We roll all four of them down. But as hot as it is, I can't persuade Niko to leave the car.

"Lemonade, Niko," I whisper to his cherry-red face.

He sinks down lower.

I finally get him out by promising a table with a view of the car.

Back in the restaurant, we order lemonade and boysenberry pie for Niko. My stomach is too upset to keep anything down, but Niko can always eat. While we're waiting for the waitress to bring our drinks, I fiddle with Dad's phone, pressing the call-back button on his last text. The call goes through.

"Mostly Reptiles," a lady answers.

The hairs on my arms suddenly spark with electricity. Niko was right. This is about snakes.

"Hello?" she asks.

"What kind of ah um business is this?"

"We supply lizards, snakes, and turtles to pet stores," she says.

"Oh," I say as Niko jumps me.

"Niko what the—"

"River! Our car!" he hollers.

Outside a tow truck is parked behind our car. A big muscular linebacker of a man in a baseball hat is sitting in the Subaru's driver's seat, changing the gearshift. He pops out and walks around to the back, loading the car on to the tow truck.

Niko dashes outside before I can stop him. I think he's going to jump this huge dude—climb him like a tree— but Niko runs right by him.

I head for the side door, then watch through the

window as the driver enters the restaurant men's room.

I'm not about to mess with that guy. He's the size of a Mack truck. Each of his hands is as big as a turkey carcass.

When I get to our car, it's already loaded on the tow truck, and Niko has climbed into the now slanted backseat. He makes a nest, burrowing low in the foot space. He pulls a beach towel over himself.

"Niko, get out of there!"

Niko ignores me.

"C'mon, the tow truck guy will be back," I plead, wondering if I should drag Niko out. I don't know if I can. He weighs twice what I did at that age. Besides, once Niko gets an idea, there's no talking him out of it. It's like the time he jumped into a motel pool from the second-story balcony because he thought a toy dinosaur was in there. It didn't matter that it wasn't our motel or his dinosaur.

"Please! Niko!" I beg.

But Niko won't budge. I can't let him go without me and I sure as heck don't want Turkey Fist to see us, so I dive into the backseat and roll myself into the foot space, across the floor hump from Niko. I pull the other beach towel over my head, panting under the hot dry towel, which smells of chlorine.

What am I doing? This is stupid. There's still time to

get Niko out of here, I think, but then the truck cab door opens. The car jiggles as the big man gets inside. The motor turns over, the cables squeak, and we begin to move.

"River," Niko whispers. "We don't have our seat belts on."

Leave it to Niko to worry about that, but I don't want him to decide to climb up and snap one on. That's just the kind of thing he'd do.

"It's okay. Dad will understand," I tell him.

"No, he won't," Niko insists, but he stays low in the footspace, the towel pulled tightly around him.

On the freeway the wind beats through the open windows, battering our towels and sending Dad's flying out. All I can think about is how to text Harpreet where to pick us up when I have no idea where we're going. I can't even tell which direction. All I see is the cloudless blue sky above me.

It's fifteen, maybe twenty minutes before we get off the highway, but we're slowing down, turning left, the pavement rising like we're pulling into a driveway. The tow wires pop, the car twists and sways as the tow truck comes to a stop. The cab door opens, the weight shifts, the door slams shut.

He's out.

Just to be sure, I wait ten beats before I look. We're pulled in to a dingy strip mall in front of an empty storefront with no sign and black-painted windows. On the left is a liquor store, on the right a pawnshop. I'm guessing the tow truck driver went into the black-windowed store, since he parked right smack in front.

Either way, we can't stay here. I'm not about to wait around for this tow truck dude to find us and crush us with his turkey fists.

"C'mon," I tell Niko.

The back of the strip mall is even dingier than the front. A Dumpster overflows with Styrofoam and wood shavings, broken lightbulbs, plastic crates, and hundreds of those little hangers that come with new socks. By the back wall, I see a buzzer with a small sign. MOSTLY REPTILES, it says.

"Bingo," I tell Niko.

"Dad's in there?" Niko whispers.

"I think so," I say.

Niko nods, his eyes dazed.

The back door is half open. Inside, I see steel girders holding shelves from floor to ceiling. On the shelves are plastic shoebox-sized boxes—maybe a hundred or more. Fans spin slowly, cutting through the hot air. Sawdust covers the floor. I'm just thinking I need our address so I can text it to Harpreet, when the door opens farther and a man with snakeskin boots, long sideburns, and a weird eye—might even be glass—repositions the doorstop.

I grab Niko and yank him behind the Dumpster, holding my breath, hoping we haven't been seen.

"Man, it's hot in here," he shouts. "When's the AC repair guy coming? We may need to unload in the alley."

We don't hear a response, but he rattles on. "Our man in Jakarta mislabeled a few frilled dragons as wild crested geckos. It can happen," Glass Eye says to someone inside. He's pacing, his voice is sometimes clear, sometimes muffled as he moves back and forth.

"And the Timor pythons he smuggled in his underwear?" Someone else asks.

"Dad?" Niko's chest rises. I can feel him start to lunge forward.

My arms tighten around him. "No!" I whisper, pressing my mouth against his hot ear. "We don't know it's safe in there."

"You can't prove that," Glass Eye says. "Not without your wire."

"Police will be here if the wire goes dead." My dad says.

Glass Eye's voice gets clearer as he paces our direction.

"What do you take me for? This is Fish and Wildlife's baby. They don't have the funding to buy toilet paper. You probably bought the wire yourself."

A delivery truck is backing through the alley. The *beep-beep* of the back-up warning makes it impossible to hear.

Glass Eye has stopped pacing. He says something I don't catch.

"You tore my house apart," my dad says when the beeping stops.

"We wanted to find out about your kids. Your older boy goes to Squaw. The younger one, Valley of the Sun. He's accident-prone anyway, isn't he?"

"You said yourself without the wire I have no proof," my father's voice is strained, like rubber bands are wrapped around his windpipe.

"You aren't known for cooperation. We thought we might need leverage."

"Don't threaten my sons!" My dad shouts.

My arms are still around Niko. I can feel him tremble.

Glass Eye whispers something back.

"Look, they know I'm here. You can't kill me," my dad's voice is loud.

Glass Eye is moving again. "What do you advise?"

"I don't have a lot of resources. You saw my car," my dad says.

"Your car is here," Glass Eye says.

"How'd you get the keys?" my dad asks.

Niko is panting like a dog. His face is so red I'm afraid he's going to pass out.

"We think out of the box. Now, I have a job for you . . . ," Glass Eyes says. "We are missing a venomous copperhead somewhere in the snake annex; got mixed up with a batch of rat snakes."

"The copperhead is valuable. You can sell him, right?" My father's voice trembles.

"Not a lot of money in venomous snakes, but I do have a customer for the copperhead, if I can locate him."

"If I die, there's going to be a—"

Glass Eye laughs before Dad can finish. "Snakebites are a rite of passage in this business."

Niko squirms out of my grasp. I tighten my grip on him. Even without hearing every word, there's no mistaking the threat.

"C'mon," I whisper, pulling him back around the strip mall.

"No, River," he says. "Dad's afraid of snakes."

"I know, but we need Harpreet," I tell him.

Niko nods. After Dad, Harpreet is his favorite person.

I check the clock on Dad's cell: 5:30. In thirty minutes, Harpreet will be out. I have to text him where we are.

The liquor store guy is Day-Glo white, like he's never been outside his store. He glares at us as if he thinks we're there to steal. When I finally get the address out of him, we run outside. My thumbs fly over the keys, texting Harpreet, but when I look up, Niko is gone.

I run around to the back door of Mostly Reptiles. The door is closed now. I try the handle . . . locked.

Oh great, they're both locked in there. Doesn't anyone think around here?

How long will it take Harpreet? Somewhere between twenty and forty minutes, I'm guessing, unless there's traffic. But Harpreet's class isn't even out yet. It might be an hour before he gets here. A lot can happen in an hour.

I try to think what I know about snakes. We have a boa in our science class. It just slithers around its cage moving slowly like a bowel movement. It eats a lot of mice though—likes them live instead of frozen. Not that I even volunteered to feed it.

Hey wait. . . . I can call the police! My dad was wearing a wire—he must have been on some secret ops mission to catch these reptile smuggler guys. Glass Eye found the wire, so there's no more mission. I slip my dad's cell out of my pocket and dial nine-one when a big turkey fist wraps around my wrist while the other hand snatches the cell.

"Who are you?" the tow truck driver booms.

"River," I mutter.

"What are you doing back here, River?"

"Looking for snakes," I say, which is kind of a lie and kind of not.

"Does this look like a pet store?"

I shrug. "Could I see what you have in there?" I ask.

"Not a chance. Get out of here, kid! Get!" He takes a drag on a cigarette, then waves it in my face, his eyes scanning the back road as if he's waiting for something.

"Can I have the cell back? It's my dad's."

"Sure, come get it," he says, holding the cell in his hand as an offering, but before I can reach it, he wraps his fingers around it and crushes it in his big turkey hand. He looks down at me, hoping for a reaction. Then he returns the smashed cell with a smile. "So you'll remember not to come back."

I take off running, like I'm scared to death, which isn't far from the truth. Turkey Fist pulverized Dad's cell in one hand. I've never seen anyone do that. I consider going into the liquor store and begging Day-Glo guy to call the police, but he was so cranky, I don't think he'd help me if I were bleeding out on his floor.

I wonder if I'll have better luck going to the front entrance. I'm about to try when I see a FedEx truck pull into the strip mall, then head around the buildings to the back.

A shipment. That's what Turkey Fist is waiting for.

I return to my hiding place behind the Dumpster. Turkey Fist props the door open, signs for the boxes, and begins unloading.

The first box has compartments like a plant nursery, but each section has a rolled-up sock. He peeks into one and dips out a small baby snake—a python maybe—which looks as if it's been dipped in white paint. He carries the box inside.

The next box has lizards with orange heads and bright green bodies. They are active, clambering to get out. This time when he goes inside, he's gone a long time. I'm guessing wherever he's taken the lizards is a considerable distance from the door. That gives me an idea. Next lizard box, I'm going in.

I have to wait through albino snakes in pillow cases and baby boa constrictors in gold-toed socks until a turquoise gecko scrambles out. This is my chance. I try not to think about what is inside Mostly Reptiles.

The smell hits me first—a strange, musty, animal smell

like eggs and dirt and burnt hair. I slip between the metal
girders of boxes, which are mostly full of mice. The sides of
the room are lined with bunny cages. But, mice and bunnies aren't reptiles.

Of course . . . they're food.

Where would Niko have gone? Where is my dad?

I duck into the dark corridor. On either side are rooms
with big glass windows. FROGS, one says. SPIDERS, another.
And then TURTLES and TORTOISES. Each room looks like
its own pet store, with wall to wall cages. I wonder where
Turkey Fist has taken the lizards. Then I spot a door that
opens to a dark passage. Above the door it says SNAKE
ANNEX.

The lights are dim in this windowless hallway; one is
flickering as if it's about to burn out. Behind me a weird
flip, flip stops me. What is that? Oh. A piece of cardboard
caught in the ceiling fan. A row of rubber gloves creep
against my arm.

The door has a small window reinforced with chicken
wire. The door creaks as I push through.

On the other side is a hallway with rooms to the left and
large chain-link cages to the right. The rooms have signs
that read SNAKES, VENOMOUS SNAKES, and LIZARDS. I think
I feel something on my leg and yank it up, but it's nothing.

Just my head messing with me. The snakes aren't out here.

I force myself to walk toward the snake room and peek in the viewing window. Oh no! Dad. He's there standing on a plastic chair, his back to me, in a sea of snakes. On the floor are snakes. Coiled in the corners, motionless in the middle, with heads tucked neatly over a coil, entwined so you can't tell mouth from tail. One moves quickly, its head rising and falling as it crosses the floor. Another tries to climb the wall, in perfect s-curves, its scales shiny like the inside of a mouth.

My father's chair is in the middle near a coiled snake tracking him with its cold reptile eyes.

I don't want to go in there.

I look at the snakes between Dad and the door. One is coiled ready to strike. Another languid, long and drawn out. What happens if you step on a venomous viper? But didn't Glass Eye say there was only one copperhead they couldn't find? But which one?

"River!" Niko's voice. He's standing in the dark back of the hall by a cage that is bigger than he is. Inside is a reptile that looks like a cross between a rhino and a lizard—it must weigh more than a hundred pounds—some kind of Gila monster on steroids. Its legs are like turtle legs and it has a weird lizard double chin and a mean snakish head and a skinny white tongue constantly flicking. I didn't know lizards came this big. Then I remember from some kid's science report . . . this is a Komodo dragon. I thought you were only supposed to have those at the zoo.

"Look! He likes hot dogs." Niko is popping hot dogs out of blankets and tossing the hot dogs in the Komodo's cage. When the Komodo locates one, he flicks it up with his tongue.

"See?" Niko smiles brightly. "He's friendly."

"Niko, no." My voice shakes.

"He likes me. He wants to come out."

"Don't!" I shout.

But Niko has already opened the cage.

"Niko." My voice dissolves down my throat. I swallow hard and try to summon it back. "Give me the hot dogs. And go in that hallway and close the door. Wait while I get Dad out."

"River . . . all of them?" Niko asks.

"Niko"—I can barely choke the words out—"I promise I'll get you more."

"Oh-kay," he sighs, handing me the Baggie. The Komodo hasn't left the cage. It's tracking Niko, its wrinkly reptile neck moving slowly, its bright brown eyes keen on my brother's shoes. It pushes out of the cage.

I toss a pig in a blanket toward the snake annex. The Komodo watches. You can almost see it thinking: *Niko or the hot dog.* The Komodo's stare returns to Niko.

I throw three more, but the Komodo has found its prey. It shoots forward low to the ground, kicking its legs sideways as it gains speed.

"Niko!" I scream. He's almost to the passage door. I take a handful of pigs in blankets and pound the Komodo. It pauses for a split second, which is all it takes for Niko to slip inside the passage. The door is closed. Niko's safe on the other side. I let my breath out in a burst.

Now suddenly the Komodo's eye is on me. My heart pounds. Adrenaline pumps through my brain as I rip toward the snake annex door, and toss the rest of the hot dogs into the room. The Komodo's head wobbles as it looks from me to the snakes. Its whole body radiates energy as it blunders into the room, focused on a snake winding up the chair leg to my father.

"Dad," I force my voice to come out quiet and calm.

"River?" Dad shouts. "Get out of here."

"Put your broom down to the left. Get the snake coming up the chair leg. Be careful," my breath runs out, "of the Komodo." I gasp.

Dad's arms shake like he has nerve damage. "I want you

safe," he sputters, jerking his broom down to the climbing snake. Is that the copperhead?

The Komodo is tracking my dad now. I toss the pig in a blanket box, but the Komodo doesn't even blink.

"Dad!" I shout, just as a viper by the wall coils and shoots toward the Komodo, its jaws wide apart. The Komodo turns, thrashing the snake, battering it, whipping the air with it until it lets go. The snake hits the wall with a thud. My father tosses his broom—and leaps. A snake shoots across the floor, its fangs open, just missing my father's bare ankle; another is motionless as my father jumps over it.

My arms are shaking so badly I can hardly get the door shut. My breath comes out in weird pants. My father's face is white as powder.

"C'mon, we have to get Niko," I tell him, heading for the passageway, picking up Niko and pulling him along. Running now through the dark hall, our feet pound the sawdust-covered floor. We fly by the bunny cages. People are yelling, but we are on fire, tearing through the building to the back door.

My dad reaches it first and yanks on the handle, but it doesn't open. He gives a long hard pull, but the handle won't budge.

Glass Eye and Turkey Fist are behind us.

"Brought your boys, did you?" Glass Eye jingles a key in his hand.

"We let the Komodo out," I tell him, my eyes on Niko. That's when it occurs to me how the metal girders of mice trays kind of look like playground equipment.

"I'm sure you did." Glass Eye's voice is thick with sarcasm.

"No, really," I say. "You better go check."

"Please," my father tells Glass Eye. "You've made your point. Let us go."

"This will be the end of your involvement?" Glass Eye asks. His real eye moving back and forth as if he's lost control of it.

"Climb," I whisper into Niko's hot ear, "then jump."

"This is Fish and Wildlife's baby, you said it yourself," my father says, as Niko climbs quick as a monkey.

"Hey!" Turkey Fist shouts, but Niko is too fast. In an instant, mice go flying—tails, feet, sawdust, water everywhere—and then Niko comes down, landing stomach first, a belly flop on Turkey Fist's large jawed head. In the chaos of Niko and the mice, I snatch the key out of Glass Eye's hand and manage to jam it in the lock. The three of us tear outside, dashing to the front, where our car has been released from the tow truck.

My father comes to an abrupt halt. "Oh no," he whispers. "The keys. They're in my laptop case."

We hear his car before we see it. His windows are rolled down; the Indian talk-radio station he loves to listen to is chattering in earnest.

"Harpreet," Niko whispers as Harpreet turns the old taxi in to the strip mall. He waves, smiles, nods his turbaned head.

We dive into his old taxi, piling in on top of one another.

"Go!" my dad shouts when he gets the door closed.

"Go, all right, Mr. James. We will go." Harpreet nods, fussing with his sun visor.

I settle back, digging between the seats for the seat belt. But my hand touches something cool and slippery, something alive. I yank it back.

"Niko." I try to get the word out, but my jaw is frozen with fear. "There's a—a—"

My dad sees it, too. His face is shiny with sweat. His skin is tinged with blue as we watch a snake crawl across Niko's lap.

Harpreet is nattering on to his taxi, giving it encouragement. "All right, little lady, we will go."

"Harpreet, stop. There's a snake," my dad whispers.

"A what, Mr. James? No. No snakes in my cab." Harpreet pounces on the brakes, and jumps out.

I don't breathe watching the brown striated snake move coil by coil, its black-ink line pupils transfixed, its head shifting from side to side as it slithers down Niko's leg. This one looks different—not like the others.

"Can I have him, Dad?" Niko asks. "Can I?"

Harpreet yanks open the passenger door, grabs the snake just behind its jaws, and sends it soaring through the parking lot.

Harpreet shakes his finger like a windshield wiper. "No snakes. Not in my cab."

My dad wipes the sweat off his chin.

My heart is still pumping loud like it lives in my ears. I shudder, thinking about that snake's weird eyes. That snake was venomous.

"Guess we found it," I say.

"Guess so," my dad whispers.

"All right, Harpreet." My dad offers a frozen smile, his eyes full of the shock of how close we came. "No snakes in your cab." He cranks down the window and gasps the outside air, which has finally begun to cool.

"And there are other things." Harpreet is ranting now.

"I do not like this business you are messing up with, Mr. James."

"Mixed up with," my father corrects.

"Mixed up with," Harpreet concedes. "'Emergency. Come now.' You scared Harpreet."

"Yeah, Dad," I say. "You scared Harpreet."

Niko doesn't say anything. He just holds my dad's hand, smiling like he has found something way better than a pig in a blanket.

"You must promise, Mr. James," Harpreet says sternly.

"They're ripping whole species out of the wild and selling them for a killing. Endangered animals, Harpreet. And nobody's stopping them because the Fish and Wildlife Department has no money."

"They have laws," Harpreet mutters.

"But no one is enforcing them. That's the point."

Harpreet's dark eyebrows furrow. "You can't catch aaaaall the bad people in the world," he mutters.

"When I see something wrong I—"

"No snakes in the cab," Harpreet interrupts. "No scaring Harpreet." He claps his hand back on the wheel.

I check my father to see how he's taking this. I've never heard Harpreet bawl him out before.

But it doesn't seem to be sinking in. I guess it's like telling

Niko to stop jumping off the top of the play structure. Niko needs to jump and my father needs to make the world a better place. But I can hope this will be the end of this . . . Can't I?

When I sleep, I dream of a thousand yellow taxis curving in a single line through the desert's dust. I wait in the hot sun to search each one for the snake.

NATE MACAVOY, MONSTER HUNTER

BY BRUCE HALE

When you show up at your best friend's house to walk to school in the morning, the last thing you expect to hear is, "Jeremy is missing." Especially if your best friend is named Jeremy.

And especially if he texted you the night before, promising to tell you about monsters.

"'Missing'?" I asked Mrs. Hyken, as we stood in the doorway. "Like, missing missing?"

She blew her bangs off her forehead and shifted Jeremy's baby sister on her hip. "What other kind of missing is there, Nate?"

"But . . ."

I knew what she meant. I just couldn't believe it.

"Have you called the cops?" I asked.

Something went *crash* in the kitchen. It sounded messy.

"Jason!" yelled Mrs. Hyken. "You better not be getting into those cookies!" Distracted, she looked away toward the ruckus. This didn't seem like the best time to mention that the baby had painted some kind of yellowish goo all over the shoulder of Mrs. Hyken's nice work outfit.

"What were we . . . ?" she said, turning back.

"The cops?" I asked again.

"Nate, honey, I don't need the cops. I know where he is."

"Where?"

Just then, Jeremy's three-year-old brother squealed and burst through the kitchen door. He made a break for the stairs, chubby fists full of cookies.

"Jason Francis Hyken, come back here!"

"You're a booty-head!" he cried.

Mrs. Hyken chased the little cookie snatcher, talking over her shoulder at me. "My snake-in-the-grass, soon-to-be-ex-husband took Jeremy." Then she used some words that had gotten me a paddling when I said them in front of my dad.

"Has he called?" I asked.

"I've left messages for both of them. But I'm sure that

dirtbag will phone me any time now to gloat. Jason, come down here this instant!"

The brat had made it up the steps. "Booty, booty, bootyhead!"

Something crashed upstairs. It sounded expensive.

The baby on Mrs. Hyken's hip began to blubber, adding snot to the other goo on Mrs. Hyken's top.

"Now, now, Jessica." She jiggled her daughter and flashed a tight smile. "Gotta go. Duty calls." Mrs. Hyken stomped upstairs.

Back outside, I nosed around for Jeremy's bike. Long gone, just like him.

Trudging the five blocks to school, I felt like I'd eaten lead waffles for breakfast. I knew Jeremy wasn't at his dad's apartment.

I knew he hadn't forgotten to tell his mom about a sleepover.

Deep in my gut, I knew the monsters had him.

Okay, before we go any further, maybe I should say a word or two about my monster "obsession," as Dad calls it. I'm not obsessed (a five-point vocabulary word, meaning totally nuts about something).

But I am fascinated.

The coolest TV show in the world, by far, is *Monster*

Hunters. Each week, Jeremy and I watch their ace investigators search for cryptids—creatures like Bigfoot, the Mothman, and the Loch Ness Monster—all over the planet.

We know cryptids like other kids know baseball players. And Jeremy and I have always, always wanted to photograph a real live cryptid. That would be our ticket onto the show, my life's ambition.

Which was why last night's message from Jeremy had me so pumped. And why his disappearance had me so worried.

I dug around in my backpack for my cell phone—a gift from Dad on my twelfth birthday the month before. Turning it on, I scrolled to our texts from last night and reread them for the tenth time:

J-Man: U won't believe what I saw!

HunterNate: What?

J-Man: Clue: Yr dreams r about 2 come true!!!

HunterNate: WHAT???

J-Man: Gotta check sumthin. Show u tomorrow!

HunterNate: WHAAAAAT????

J-Man: Yr favorite thing.

HunterNate: CRYPTIDS???

J-Man: O, maybe :)

HunterNate: Tell me!!!

J-Man: L8er, dude!

That told me a whole bunch of nothing useful. What was he going to check on? Where had he found this thing? And what the heck had he found?

Jeremy knew my big dream, so his secret had to be connected with cryptids. But how could that be?

Seriously, what kind of cryptid would hang out in a blah little suburb like Whippleboro, Massachusetts—the Mall Monster? The Abominable Snowblower Man? The Creature from the Stinkety Skating Rink?

And what, exactly, was it doing with my best friend?

My thoughts whirled as I shuffled to school in a daze. I wanted to go grab my bike and start looking for Jeremy, but without knowing what he'd found, I had no clue where to start.

Besides, as a passing cop car reminded me, grown-ups generally frown on kids ditching school.

Wait—a cop car?

"Hey!" I shouted. I waved my hands and ran after it, book bag thumping against my back. "Stop! Help! Come back!"

A half block later, the black-and-white pulled over to the curb ahead of me. The window buzzed down on the passenger side, and a beefy white guy with a furry caterpillar mustache leaned out.

"What's the problem, kid?"

"It's . . . my friend," I panted. "He's . . . missing."

"Oh, yeah?" said Officer Mustache. His eyes hid behind dark sunglasses. The caterpillar on his lip twitched. "How long?"

"Since, uh . . ." Now that I thought of it, Mrs. Hyken hadn't told me when Jeremy disappeared. "Since last night."

Officer Mustache looked over at his partner, a lean black woman with a serious expression and shades to match.

"What do your friend's parents say?" she asked.

"His, uh, mom says she thinks Jeremy's dad took him—"

"Uh-huh," said Officer Serious.

"But I think something else—um, someone else—got him. Please, can't you start looking?"

The cops traded another glance.

"D-I-V-O-R-C-E," said Officer Serious, as if I couldn't spell for beans.

"Yup," said Officer Mustache. He turned back to me. "Has his mom filed a report?"

"No."

"Then there's nothing we can do."

I clenched my fists in frustration. "But I just know

something's wrong. Please?"

Officer Serious shot me a look. "Go to school, kid. He'll probably be back home by the time you are."

I pulled out all the stops, giving them the ol' lost-my-puppy stare. "Please?"

Two pairs of sunglasses stared back, like the eyes of two giant bugs dressed in blue. The window buzzed up, and the car rolled away.

Shoot.

I shifted my book bag on my shoulders. So the police wouldn't do anything? Fine. I'd rescue Jeremy myself. I'd—

Brrrriinnnng! went the bell.

—do it right after school.

The morning's classes passed in a blur. All through math and social studies, I kept turning over the problem in my head. How could I figure out where Jeremy had gone?

By the time the lunch bell rang, I knew where to start. I wolfed down my county fair dog and potato salad and hit the library.

The librarian, Mrs. Kunkle, sat in her office, eating macaroni from a takeout container and staring blankly into space, like she was on screen-saver mode. I waved. She waved back, without shifting her eyes or slowing down her fork.

Just my luck, one of the computers was free. I opened the web browser and typed CRYPTID WHIPPLEBORO MA into the search engine.

Bam. 55,681 hits.

Great.

I took about ten minutes checking out the websites. Normally, I loved this stuff and could spend my whole lunch hour reading it. But not today. I couldn't stop thinking of Jeremy, captured somewhere, with monsters standing over him drooling.

Right away I skipped all of the ghost-related websites. Serious monster hunters don't believe in ghosts.

I zeroed in on true cryptids. The Dover Demon looked promising—huge orange eyes, watermelon head, makes bloodcurdling noises. But Dover was at least three hours' drive away.

I kept searching.

Pukwudgies caught my eye next. Goofy name. But these cryptids were anything but goofy. Pukwudgies are gray, troll-like creatures that can appear and disappear at will. They can change themselves into different animals; they've been sighted all over Massachusetts.

And, according to Wampanoag tribal legends, they love playing nasty tricks on humans.

I scanned page after page. But I couldn't find any helpful

details on Pukwudgies, like where they hung out, what
they did with kidnapped kids, or how you dealt with them
once you found them.

There had to be someone I could ask. . . .

Duh.

Of course! If the staff of my favorite TV show didn't
know more about Pukwudgies than anyone around, I'd eat
my book bag (or the cafeteria's mystery meat, whichever
was worse).

I got the *Monster Hunters* phone number from their
website. Stepping outside, I punched the digits into my cell
phone. True, Dad had said to use it only for emergencies,
but if this wasn't an emergency, what was?

After five rings, a bored-sounding woman's voice said,
"*Monster Hunters*, no cryptid too cryptic. How can I help
you?"

"Um, I . . ." Now that the moment had arrived, I choked.
This woman could connect me with one of the monster
hunters. I might even end up talking with Ace Gronsteen
himself.

"Whaddaya want, kid?"

I cleared my throat. "Can I, uh, talk to one of the monster hunters?"

"Regarding what?"

"Um, Pukwudgies. I need anything they can tell me."

The woman grunted. Her hand must have covered the phone, because next I heard a brief, muffled conversation. She came back on.

"They're not available right now."

I gripped the phone. "When will they be?"

"I could take a message," she said, sounding like she'd rather jam a sharp pencil into her eyeball.

"This is important!" I snapped. "A kid's life is at stake."

A rusty-sounding chuckle leaked from the phone. "Good one. So, someone's gonna kill you if you don't turn in your cryptid report on time?"

"No, it's my friend. He—"

"Thanks for watching, kid. See ya."

The line went dead.

I sagged against the redbrick wall of the library. My mind spun around and around. And like a silver ball in one of those arcade games, it finally went down the last hole left.

I gulped.

Only one person could tell me what I needed to know.

And that one person was the toughest kid in sixth grade.

Brandon Frye.

Normally, Brandon is the last guy you'd go looking for. He's built like a big brown refrigerator, with a shock of thick black hair, eyes like black lasers, and the sweet disposition of a hungry wolverine.

Even teachers get nervous around him.

But Brandon was the only part-Wampanoag person I knew. If anyone at school could fill me in on Pukwudgies, it would be him.

Finding Brandon wasn't a problem. Lunchtimes, he usually hung out with his girlfriend and some other tough kids on the benches by the baseball diamond.

Talking to him was the problem.

I stuffed my hands into my jeans pockets and drifted toward the benches, pretending to watch some kids playing pickle out on the field.

Brandon and his friends laughed at some joke. Hearing that, I thought, *Good mood*, and turned around.

"Hi, uh, Brandon," I said.

The laughter stopped like someone threw a switch. Brandon Frye, his two weasel-like buddies, and his red-haired girlfriend all stared at me.

"Nice day, huh?" I squeaked.

"Nice day for a pounding," said the first weasel guy. Weasel Number Two snickered. Brandon kept staring.

"I know you?" he rumbled. The guy's voice was as low as a high schooler's.

"We were in fourth grade together?" I said. "Now we're

in Mr. Sarner's science class?" I'm not sure why everything I said came out like a question.

"You're Nick," he said.

"It's, uh, Nate, actually."

He shook his massive head. "Nick."

I shrugged. "Okay; Nick. Listen, can we talk?"

"All Brandon wants to hear from you is, 'Here's my lunch money,'" said Weasel Number One.

I held my palms up. "Already spent it. I just want some information."

Brandon cocked his head and narrowed his eyes, considering me. He spat.

"What'll you pay?"

"Pay?"

"Yeah," he said. "I answer your questions, I'm givin' you something. What'll you give me?"

I dug in my pockets. Nothing but lint and odd scraps of paper.

"What do you want?"

Brandon chuckled. "What do I want? A million bucks, a new house for my family, to win the Ultimate Fighting Smackdown, and for losers to stop calling me 'Injun.'"

The weasel guys laughed and bumped fists. The redheaded girl swatted his arm in that funny way that girls do.

"What do I want from you?" Brandon stood, towering

over me. The sun disappeared behind his head.

I gulped.

"A game of flinch."

"What?" Flinch was a dumb game the guys at my school played. Basically, if you made the other person flinch, you got to slug them on the shoulder.

"Yeah," said Brandon Frye. "For every question, we play one round. Deal?"

"Deal."

I thought for a bit, wanting to get my questions just right. Too few, and I wouldn't find Jeremy. Too many, and I'd lose the use of my arm.

"Okay," I said. "First question: if we had Pukwudgies living in the area, where would I find them?"

Brandon's forehead crinkled, and he gave a disbelieving smirk. "Pukwudgies? You been talkin' to my grandma?"

Weasel Number One looked confused. "What's a Puckawuddie?"

"Only a nasty little troll that likes to push people off cliffs," said Brandon, making claws of his hands. He feinted at his friends, who chuckled nervously. "And you want to find a Pukwudgie?" he asked me.

I nodded.

"You crazy, Nick." He gave an elaborate shrug. "But if they exist, they like caves, tunnels, that sort of place.

That's what Grandma says."

Quick as a snake striking, Brandon jammed two fingers toward my eyes.

I blinked and moved back.

"Flinch!" He grabbed my right arm with one meaty fist and pounded my shoulder, hard, with the other.

"Ow!" After he let go, I rubbed my sore arm.

The weasel guys hooted.

"Next question," I said. "Do Pukwudgies have any weaknesses?"

Brandon walked around me, rubbing his jaw. "Let's see . . . from what I remember, they like strawberry bread."

"Strawberry shortcake?" the redheaded girl asked.

He arched a dark eyebrow. "You think the old-time Wampanoag had shortcake and whipped cream? Nah, strawberry bread—like banana bread, but with straw-berries."

"Anything else?" I asked.

Brandon snapped his fingers. "And water. They make some kinda magic fire, so they don't like water."

"Magic fi— Aaugh!" The up-close-and-personal sight of Brandon's fist whooshing toward my nose turned my question into a shout.

"Flinched again," he sang. This time, Brandon wound

up like a home-run slugger. His mighty punch zoomed straight for my poor shoulder, and at the last second, he turned it into a little tap.

Uproarious laughter from his sidekicks.

Never mind that he'd already mangled me. I held my arm protectively and wondered if Jeremy would come visit me in the hospital.

Assuming, of course, that I managed to find him.

Brandon smirked and rubbed his knuckles into his palm. "Any other questions, Nick?"

Which way to the emergency room? came to mind, but I didn't say it. "No, that's all. Thanks for the, uh, help."

He spread his hands. "Anytime. Come on, guys."

The weasel dudes and the redhead ambled off after Brandon. They looked like pilot fish trailing a tiger shark.

About twenty feet off, Brandon Frye turned. "Hey, Nick!"

"Yeah?" I called.

His dark eyes turned serious. "Watch yourself with those Pukwudgies. They make me look like a Girl Scout."

Weasel Number Two started to snicker, until Brandon showed him his fist. That shut him up.

A softball rolled across the grass and stopped near my feet.

"A little help?" cried one of the guys playing pickle.

I cocked my foot and kicked it to him. Ball tossing would have to wait until I got some feeling back into my arm.

By the time the last bell rang, I had patched together a plan. Sort of. I felt a bit nervous about facing a bunch of evil trolls on my own, so I went for backup.

Leaving school, I spotted Kellen Bradley waiting at the curb for his ride. Perfect. He was a sort-of friend, the tallest boy in our grade (next to Brandon), and a total jock.

"Hey, Kellen."

He jerked his chin at me. "Whassup, Nate?"

"I'm, uh, going on a little adventure."

His eyebrows rose. "Oh, yeah?"

"Yeah. Jeremy kind of got himself into a tight spot, so I'm gonna go rescue him. Wanna come?"

The eyebrows came back down. "Is it dangerous?"

I shrugged. "Um, a little bit. Maybe."

"Gee, I'd really like to. But I've got karate class."

"See, that's why I thought you—"

"And here's my ride."

A blue-gray SUV pulled up to the curb. Kellen opened the passenger door and slipped inside. "Sorry, Nate. See ya."

And the car drove off.

On the walk home, I called my dad.

"Hey, buddy, what's up?"

"Are you busy?"

He chuckled. "Yeah, I'm slammed. We've got that big meeting, and I won't be home until late, remember? What's going on?"

Shoot. Although Dad was pretty open-minded about my "cryptid hobby," I doubted he'd blow off a major meeting to go monster hunting.

"Uh, nothing, I guess. Hey, can I take some money from the cookie jar for a snack?"

"Sure thing, buddy. Just don't max out on the sweets."

"I won't. Dad, I—"

"Yes, Nate?"

I shook my head. "Nothing. See you later."

We hung up. I'd almost told him I loved him. That was nuts. This was just going to be a quick in and out—find Jeremy, grab Jeremy, run like heck. No big deal.

Right?

So why was my stomach doing flip-flops?

It took about fifteen minutes to collect everything I needed and stuff it into my book bag. Then I rode my bike to the supermarket and picked up the last items.

Assuming Jeremy had seen Pukwudgies, and assuming that's who had him now, and also assuming Brandon hadn't lied—a lot of assumptions—I was left with two likely places to search.

The caves and the storm drains.

I really hoped it wasn't the storm drains. They gave me the creeps. Many times, Jeremy had tried to talk me into exploring them, and I'd always found an excuse not to.

Until now.

But the drains—big concrete tunnels that sluiced rainwater away from the town—were much closer than the caves. So that's where I went first.

A cold breeze whipped through my jacket as I pedaled past the last houses and out to the Little League diamonds. The season was over. The grass had turned brown, and that metal thingy on the rope kept striking the empty flagpole with a lonely *ting, ting, ting.*

I was all alone.

A deep gully snaked around the outer edge of the far diamond. At its widest bend lay the hungry mouth of the storm drain.

Oh, boy.

I leaned my bike against an oak tree, hefted my book bag, and stepped over to the edge of the gully. I promised myself I'd take a look—just a look—before moving on to check out the caves.

"He's probably not here," I muttered.

Scrambling down the bank, I was thankful that it hadn't rained for a week. Only a trickle of water burbled down the gully. But it was enough to create a wide muddy spot at the edge of the concrete apron.

Tracks crisscrossed the mud. Tennis shoes, dog and raccoon prints, and the traces of something my old Cub Scouts training hadn't covered.

The tracks looked like those of a barefoot human, only wider. But with claw marks. And only four toes.

A shiver danced down my spine.

I sighted along the footprints, and they seemed to head straight for the black, gaping mouth of a tunnel. The storm drain.

Something orange caught my eye. Then I saw it—up behind the bushes on the opposite bank: Jeremy's bike.

Great. He must have hidden it there when he went to investigate.

And now it was my turn.

I checked my watch. Maybe an hour of daylight left. I wiped my palms on my jeans. Something in my gut told me I really didn't want to be down in the tunnels when night fell.

Hands patted pockets for a final check. Flashlight. Cell phone. Pocketknife. Squirt gun.

I was as ready as I'd ever be.

"Stop stalling," I mumbled, approaching the rusty metal grille that blocked the tunnel mouth.

My hands gripped the cold iron bars.

Probably won't open, I thought. *Probably rusted shut.*

A firm tug, and the grille swung upward with a moan.

I flinched so violently, Brandon could've slugged me three times.

So much for the element of surprise. I flicked on the flashlight, squeezed under the grille, and stepped into a puddle of water.

Shoot. Galoshes. I *knew* I'd forgotten something.

The flashlight beam played over a concrete tunnel a little taller than me, walls stained dark with water, and floor covered in rubbish and rocks. After about twenty feet, the glow of my light was swallowed by pitch black.

I gulped.

On one wall, in red, some joker had spray-painted a skull and crossbones over a message:

KEEP OUT, DUMMY!

Good advice. I ignored it.

Taking a deep breath, I crept forward, one hand on the flashlight, one on the side wall for balance. My every footfall echoed and reechoed.

A faint cabbagey odor mingled with the rich smells of

earth and water. Now and then, I got a whiff of some animal's poop. Ripe.

About fifty feet in, I turned to look back. The entrance had shrunk to a circle of light about the size of my fist.

My heart thudded unevenly. *Just a nice little underground stroll*, I told myself. *Nothing to get spooked about.*

Right.

I pushed on. Not far ahead, more of the creepy-looking tracks crossed a patch of mud. A faint light spilled from above. Craning my neck, I saw a shaft with a grille at the top. I figured I was under a street.

Splashing echoed in the tunnel ahead. I pointed the flashlight. Red eyes glowed in the dark.

"Aaugh!" I jumped.

Then I relaxed.

Trapped in my beam was a fat raccoon. It grumbled at me. But when I chucked a rock in its direction, the animal hissed and retreated down a side tunnel.

When I reached the passage, I shined the light down it. The raccoon was nowhere to be seen.

Weird.

I continued down the main tunnel. A minute later, the smooth concrete pipe ended. From here, the passage was made of individual stone blocks fitted together like a wall.

It looked really old, like Pilgrims old.

Pukwudgie territory.

I moved slower, trying to keep quiet. The tunnel curved, then widened into a section where big stone pillars held up the roof. Lots of the strange footprints crisscrossed the muddy floor.

Another side tunnel led off to the right, glowing faintly from deep inside. I heard a distant chuckling, like an underground stream or far-off voices—it was hard to tell which.

The flashlight beam revealed a regular Pukwudgie freeway of footprints headed this way.

I shrugged the book bag off my shoulders and took out the white bread and strawberries. Then I crept to the far end of this wide chamber, opened the packages, and started making strawberry sandwiches, smooshing the fruit to release its smell.

I laid the sandwiches on some sheets of notebook paper. *Come and get it!* Then I tiptoed back and stepped behind a pillar, close by the entrance to the side passage.

Off went the flashlight. I crouched against the column to wait.

Time passed. I didn't know how much.

I thought about how dumb I'd feel if the raccoon returned and ate the sandwiches.

I thought about how scared I'd feel if I was still down here at night.

The darkness crowded in. The weight of all that earth above me seemed to press down like a giant hand. I could picture the ceiling collapsing and burying me under the rocks, so archaeologists from some future time would find my bleached bones.

This is why I'm not so crazy about tunnels.

My fingernails dug into my palms. I opened my eyes wide, but all I could see was more darkness.

Then, a faint light. Were my eyes playing tricks?

Slowly, steadily, it strengthened, bringing the far wall into focus—as if the glow came from the side tunnel. Stealthy little shuffling accompanied the light.

I held my breath.

Something passed by on the other side of the pillar. Ever so sneakily, I peeked around the corner.

A possum?

The raspy-looking, gray-furred beast waddled along, sniffing the air. It caught scent of the strawberries and perked right up. Then, it scampered toward the far side of the chamber, much faster than a possum could move.

When it reached the feast, it raised a weird cry.

That cry was echoed in the side tunnel. And suddenly,

a dozen or more creatures hurried past, following the possum.

The hair on my neck stood up.

Light from the torches they carried revealed gray-skinned, muscular, potbellied creatures. Their hair hung long and matted, their noses and ears were grotesquely huge, and their long fingers reminded me of spider legs. The creatures stank of wet dog and cabbage.

They looked like something from a particularly nasty fairy tale.

Pukwudgies.

The creatures stood maybe a foot shorter than me. But I wouldn't want to face one in a dark tunnel, let alone a dozen. The last of the bunch descended on the strawberry feast, jabbering and arguing in their strange tongue.

The possum turned into another Pukwudgie.

Cool! My very first cryptids. I reached for my cell phone to photograph them.

And then I remembered where I was.

Time to move.

Heart hammering like crazy, I tiptoed around the pillar and into the side passage. The torches' glow petered out after about ten feet, so I cautiously switched on my flash-light, shielding the beam with my fingers.

The floor was clear of rubble, so I hustled along as quietly as I could. Up the tunnel, around a bend, and suddenly, there I was.

A high-ceilinged cavern opened up before me. Glittering stalactites hung from above. Torches lit a comfortable crash pad for trolls. Stolen blankets lined sleeping nooks, pilfered plates rested on a flat rock by a fire pit.

And on the other side of the pit, a sad figure slumped, tied with ropes to a stone pillar.

"Jeremy!" I hissed.

His head snapped up. "Nate?"

Jeremy's glasses were askew, his curly hair was full of dirt and twigs, and his clothes were a muddy mess. But he was alive!

"Nate! You—"

"Shhh!" I dashed to his side. "They'll hear you," I whispered.

I opened the pocketknife and began sawing at his ropes.

"How did you find me?"

I sat back on my heels. "Through some genius investigative work, actually. See, I figured you were after a cryptid, so I went on the web and searched for—"

"More cutting, less talking." Jeremy shot a worried glance at the tunnel mouth.

"Right."

Before long, I had sawed through the last rope. I helped

Jeremy to stand. Together, we made our way across the chamber to the exit tunnel and started down the passage.

"Seriously, dude," Jeremy whispered. "How'd you find me?"

"You texted me about cryptids."

"No, I didn't."

With my free hand, I fished my cell phone from my pocket and handed it to him. "Look at our messages."

He punched several buttons. "Where's the . . . ?"

"Here, let me." As we kept walking, I called up the menu and opened the saved texts. "See?"

Jeremy scrolled through them. "I never actually said I'd found a cryptid. And especially not—"

We stepped out of the side tunnel and nearly bumped into a pack of . . .

"Pukwudgies!" we screamed.

"Gaaahhh!" the savage trolls screamed back.

In that frozen moment, every detail stood out like on high-def TV. The beady black eyes of the creatures. Their honking big noses, their batlike ears, the smears of red fruit on their faces and beards.

The sharp claws on their long, grasping fingers.

I had time to think, *We are so dead*.

Click went the camera flash on my cell phone.

Then, poof! They disappeared.

Jeremy and I exchanged a brief, confused look.

"Yahhh!" we cried, rushing forward in a blind panic.

I thudded into two or three invisible bodies. Hands snatched at me, but I blew through them.

With Jeremy right behind, I barreled up that dim tunnel as fast as I could go. Around the bend, back into the smooth concrete pipe we ran.

Angry hisses and unearthly growls filled the dark behind us, echoing off the walls. Many footsteps pounded.

"Faster!" Jeremy shouted.

We dashed past the raccoon's side tunnel, past the shaft leading up to the street.

I stumbled over a rock and pitched forward. Only Jeremy's swift grab kept me from doing a face-plant.

"Hurry!" he cried. "They're catching up!"

"This *is* hurrying!"

The tunnel entrance appeared ahead—a faint, small circle.

I ran like I'd never run before. My breath came in ragged gasps, my side ached like someone had stabbed me with a hot knife.

With agonizing slowness, the entrance grew bigger.

The Pukwudgies' footfalls were deafening; it sounded

like an army was running right behind us. No way could we beat them to the tunnel mouth.

And then, twenty feet from the entrance, the sound of pursuit stopped dead.

All I could hear was Jeremy's and my footsteps.

"Do you . . . think they . . . gave up?" I panted.

"Dunno."

We slowed enough for me to shine the flashlight behind us.

The dark exploded with chittering. Winged bodies rushed straight at us.

"Bats!"

"*Vampire* bats?" cried Jeremy.

Electrified by fear, we bolted for the entrance, jamming through the tunnel side by side.

"Me first," grunted Jeremy.

"No, me!"

Together we hit the iron grille like the front four of the Green Bay Packers.

Bam!

It swung upward. Bats swept past our shoulders, through our hair.

"Eeeauugh!" Jeremy yelled.

The flying rodents spilled through the gaps in the grille

and out into the cool twilight air.

We staggered forward onto the concrete apron. My shoe caught on a rock, and this time I did go down—*plonk!*—face-first into the mud.

I rolled over, arms raised to protect myself from the killer bat attack.

But no attack came.

The bats fluttered past us and dispersed into the gathering night.

"Were those Pukwudgies," said Jeremy, helping me up, "or real bats?"

I looked at the tunnel, then at the bats. "Either way, let's beat it."

We grabbed our bikes and pumped like crazy for home, setting a new speed record in the process. In fact, we didn't slow down until we turned off Brainerd Street onto my block.

Full dark had fallen on the neighborhood, but high above, the sky was still the blue of your oldest pair of jeans. The happy clatter of families making dinner drifted from nearby houses.

We stopped at the foot of my driveway.

"Well," said Jeremy. "That happened."

"Yeah. But who'd believe us?"

A grin tugged at the corners of his mouth. "Only the whole world, dude."

"What?"

Jeremy pulled my cell phone from his jacket, and I remembered the accidental flash that startled the Pukwudgies.

"Let me see!" My hands were trembling. The world of cryptid hunters is full of terrible, blurry photos that don't prove anything (other than that the person who took them was a lousy photographer).

Would our shot be any different?

I scrolled through my photo library to the last one taken.

And there it was. Blurry and dim, but you could just make out the startled faces of two Pukwudgies—honking big noses, beady eyes, and all.

"Sweet!" said Jeremy.

I smiled. But then I looked closer. Behind the trolls, caught in the flash's glare, I saw something I'd never expected, not in a million years.

"Uh-oh," I said.

"Is that—?" said Jeremy.

And I knew our monster adventure was only beginning.

BOYS WILL BE BOYS
BY JAMES PATTERSON

As soon as they boarded the light rail at the Mount Washington stop, the two boys got as far away as they could from everyone else in their class. They squeezed in beside an old lady in a Mets hat, who gave them a sour glance.

Fred was laughing himself goofy.

Will pushed his shoulder. "Shut up."

Fred continued to snort. "You are totally into her," he choked out between gasps. "Totally."

"Shut. Up," said Will, punching Fred's arm.

"That's okay," said Fred. "She is pretty hot. If you like weight lifters."

Will punched Fred again. Harder this time. "I said, shut

up!" He edged away and pulled out his DS, wishing Fred would leave him alone for once. They had been best friends all their lives, but there were times—and this was one of them—when being friends with Fred was more trouble than it was worth.

Fred seemed to get the message, which was unusual for him. He slid over a little himself, and started humming.

Will tried not to listen to what Fred was humming, but pretty soon he realized that the song was "I Kissed a Girl." Fred started laughing again. Will gave Fred one more slug and got up to sit in the front of the car. Fred could be such a jerk sometimes.

The train stopped at Cold Spring Avenue. Two older guys got on. Will sort of thought he recognized them. They looked to be about his brother's age—somewhere in high school. They must have played in some game against his brother's school. But they didn't look like athletes. They looked like trouble. They smelled like a bad combination of cigarettes and BO. They each grabbed two greasy metal handholds hanging down from the ceiling right behind Will. They swung on the handholds like a couple of apes.

The big and fat guy with the greasy mop of hair around his head was laughing so hard he started coughing. "Oh man, if Narky and Deke pull this off, this is going to be *awesome*," he said. "How long till we get there?"

"Quiet," said the little wiry one. He was definitely more dangerous-looking. He scanned the train car and caught Will staring at them. He looked daggers back at Will, which made Will gulp, go sweaty, and turn away, trying to shrink into the corner. But Will couldn't stop checking them out in spite of himself.

Will saw the little ape hitch his head to the side, motioning to the big ape to move farther down the car. They shuffled back until they stood hanging right over Fred. The little guy gave Fred the eye. Fred got the message and got up, taking the handholds himself. The two apes squeezed onto the bench where Fred and Will had been sitting. They put their heads together, talking in low voices. Will kept watching them carefully out of the corner of his eye. Every few seconds, Big Ape would snort and laugh and put up his fist for a bump from Little Ape, who would return the gesture after a second.

Will walked to the front of the car until he was standing right behind the glass partition where the driver sat. He was trying to get as far away from the apes as possible, but Fred stayed put. Will noticed he was looking around the train car as though his mind was somewhere else. But Will knew better. Fred was pretty lame some of the time, but he was one of the world's best eavesdroppers. He learned stuff from listening around lockers and desks that no one knew. Will remembered why he liked hanging out with his friend.

After a few moments, Fred made his way to the front of the car. He stood next to Will with his back to the apes. He said in a low voice, "Don't look now, but do you know those two guys who just got on?"

Will took a quick glance back over Fred's shoulder. "Yeah, I'm not sure who they are," he whispered. "But they're creeping me out."

"They're setting up some kind of gigantic prank or something," said Fred. "They keep casing out the train. And the big guy keeps saying stuff like, 'Gonna be Crazy Town!' and 'Old farts gonna drop like flies!'"

Will swallowed nervously and turned back toward the driver. "Do you think they're going to pull the emergency brake?"

"Maybe," said Fred, turning back himself. "But it sounds like something bigger than that."

"Do you think we should tell someone?" said Will.

"Tell them what?" said Fred. "That two guys are laughing about something? What would they even do? And what if those guys find out we tried to get them in trouble?"

"Yeah, you're right," said Will, turning back quickly again, in spite of himself—just long enough to see Little Ape giving him the Glance of Death. Will almost peed his pants.

The train pulled into the Woodbury stop and Will and Fred huddled forward to avoid the crush of new passengers. After some silent jostling, the bell sounded and the train slipped back into gear.

Through the glass partition at the front of the car, the boys watched the driver adjust the train's speed, then take out his cell phone.

"When I was little I really wanted to be a train engineer," said Fred, which Will took to mean he was trying to change the subject.

"When did you decide being a dork would be more fun?"

"The same time you realized you'd rather be a benchwarmer than an actual baseball player," said Fred.

The driver nudged forward a black-handled lever.

"How much do you think you make as a train engineer?" asked Fred.

"I bet sixty thousand, starters," said Will. "That's pretty skilled work."

"More than a teacher?"

"Ask him," said Will, pointing at the driver on the other side of the glass.

"No, you," said Fred.

"I don't care how much he gets paid. It looks insanely boring," said Will.

"I don't think so," said Fred.

"Then how come more people don't want to do it?" said Will.

"I bet lots of people want to do it; it's just there aren't that many openings. I mean, how many trains are there?" said Fred.

"There are a lot more in Europe," said Will. He'd just returned from a family trip to France and thought he needed to mention it at least once every five minutes. "Here, everyone drives cars."

"Anybody can drive a car," said Fred. "Driving a train could be so much cooler. Who ever ran around saying they wanted to grow up and be a car driver?"

"Race-car drivers," said Will.

"Yeah, but that's different. I mean regular drivers, just like regular train drivers; there aren't any race-train drivers." Fred laughed. "Are there?"

"Just this guy," said Will.

"And he's got the skills to do it blindfolded," said Fred.

The driver was looking down at his phone, entirely oblivious to the tracks ahead.

"Well, I guess there's no steering wheel to worry about," said Will.

The white concrete ties blurred at the bottom frame of the window, and the lush vegetation blurred past on either side like it was coming off two freely spinning bolts of fabric. The boys jostled sideways as the train took another bend in the tracks.

"Smash left!" said Fred, laughing.

"Get off!" said Will, grabbing at Fred's T-shirt to keep from falling. The track straightened and deposited the train in a long, green valley traversed by two lofty highway overpasses.

Fred was watching the driver—still looking at his phone—so Will saw the man first. The curve in the tracks had hidden him from view but now there he was—dressed in jeans and what looked like a hooded bubble jacket, lying facedown across the tracks so that his legs were over one rail and his shoulders and neck across the other. If he knew there was a train coming, he wasn't doing anything about it.

Will tried to yell, but the best he could manage was to grab Fred's arm and shake him.

"Hey!" yelled Fred, looking first at his nearly paralyzed friend and then to where Will was staring—out the front window. He saw the body and yelled himself. The driver jerked his head up.

One of the body's arms was bent strangely and the hand—rigid and pale in the slanting morning sunlight—was thrust upward behind its back.

"It's too late," Fred whispered.

The horn bleated and the train shuddered violently as the driver finally hit the brakes. The already off-balance boys were thrown up against the glass—they almost couldn't have looked away if they'd tried. Fred was right: there was no way he could stop the train in time to keep it from crushing the man on the tracks.

It was all over in a few seconds. The man was quickly and—below the shuddering din of the decelerating train—silently sucked underneath.

"No!" Fred and Will both yelled.

The train lurched to a stop. Fred and Will looked at each other. They couldn't believe what they'd just seen. They were so shocked that they almost didn't catch the glimpse of color out the window, just off the edge of the tracks—two guys in hooded, purple-and-black football jackets clambering away up over the crest of the wooded incline to the right of the rail bed.

Fred whispered, "What the . . ."

Will realized he was still gripping Fred's arm with all his strength. He let go and slid down onto the ridged-rubber floor of the train car, trying to fight back tears.

The driver shut off the horn. Fred looked down at Will.

"Maybe he was unconscious or even dead already," said Fred. "I didn't see him move at all."

"Gonna . . . be . . . sick," gasped Will.

"Breathe deep," said Fred, patting his friend on the back.

The driver had been bent over his console, entirely motionless until he heard Fred's voice. He turned and addressed him through the partition.

"You see that?" he asked.

Fred nodded.

"Can you keep quiet for a bit?" said the driver. "Dispatch will see we're stopped and the police will come, but it's important not to panic the passengers while we wait."

Fred nodded again.

The driver turned back to his control panel and spoke briefly into his cell phone. Then he took his seat and swiveled the silver articulated microphone to his mouth.

His voice crackled throughout the train.

"Attention, passengers. We are being held momentarily

by the dispatcher. Please remain in your seats and be patient. Apologies for the sudden stop. If anyone was hurt, please stay where you are and someone will be with you shortly."

An annoyed, speculative buzz rose through the train compartment. "What's wrong with the kid up front?" someone said.

The old lady in the Mets hat had toppled out of her seat and was lying on the floor holding her shoulder and groaning. A couple of other people reached out to help her but she cried, "Don't touch me! You'll make it worse!"

Fred and Will looked back at the commotion. They both saw Big Ape and his Little Ape pal moving to the back of the train. The little guy turned like he knew they were watching. He gave them one intense stare, and then disappeared into the milling crowd.

Soon the car was filled with the Mets hat lady's moans. Some other people in the compartment were rubbing their foreheads or arms where they had bumped the seat backs. Fred and Will's social studies teacher, Mr. Brown, found them at the front of the train.

"Are you guys all right?" he said, holding Will's shoulder and looking them both over. "Are you hurt?"

"No," said Will, his eyes big and staring. The driver told

them to not say anything, but did he mean to not say anything to their teacher even?

The police arrived within a few minutes. The driver exited and locked his compartment. He produced a cookie-cutter key and inserted it into the recessed lock next to the right-side doors. They folded open, and a middle-aged officer appeared at the foot of the stairs. He looked up at the driver, somberly.

"That stiff," he said, "was stiff."

"He was dead already?" asked the driver.

The cop shook his head somberly.

"Stiffer than that."

"What?"

The officer cracked a smile. "It was a freakin' mannequin!"

"What?" repeated the driver.

"A department store mannequin."

The driver collapsed back against the wall, folded his arms across his chest, and shook his head.

"Did you see anyone around?" asked the policeman.

The driver shook his head.

Fred looked at Will. Will looked at Fred. If they didn't say anything, no one would ever know they saw anybody. They would go on their way to their field trip. The guys in the purple-and-black football jackets would go on with their lives.

"Pretty sick idea for a joke," said the policeman. "You have to wonder who would pull a stunt like that. Does somebody hate you, train guy?"

The driver shook his head again. He still looked dazed.

Fred realized this might mess with this guy's mind for a long time. Fred nodded to Will. Will said, "We saw some kids running up the hill over there."

The policeman turned to him coolly. "How many?"

"Two," said Will quietly.

"We were standing up front here," explained Fred. "We saw them run off into the woods."

"Well, I guess you two get to stay behind for questioning then," he said.

"I'll stay with you guys," said Mr. Brown. "Mrs. Balzer and Mrs. Bray can handle the field trip."

Another officer, a woman, stepped up behind them.

"Should we ask the cattle if they saw anything, Jake?"

"Well, these two said they did. Go ahead and do a quick sweep while you and Taylor check for injuries. Anyone who saw anything or anyone with a boo-boo gets off here. Otherwise I don't see any reason why the train can't keep going."

"I was supposed to swap out of my shift down at the yard," said the driver. "You want to interview me there?"

"Mount Royal depot? Sure. We'll meet you outside." He turned to the boys. "Come on, you two. You see that cruiser over there? Officer Kronsky will take your statements."

"I'll get my bag and meet you there," said Mr. Brown. The policeman nodded.

Outside the train, some plainclothes policemen went onto the tracks, picking up and bagging the scattered plastic-and-wire pieces of the demolished dummy.

"Great," said Will as he and Fred went down the train steps toward Officer Kronsky's cruiser. "Now we're going to miss the field trip and everything."

Fred ignored the complaint. "I kind of knew it wasn't a person. It didn't look natural, you know."

"Well, I didn't know it wasn't a person," said Will. "Who would do something like that?"

The minute he said it, Will remembered Little Ape and Big Ape. Will looked at Fred and knew what he was thinking.

"Those guys who got on at Cold Spring?" said Will.

Fred stopped on the slope of the crushed-stone siding. "This had to be it. This was the big prank."

"Oh man," said Will, looking at the police cruiser. "We

can tell the cops about the football-jacket guys. But if we tell them about the ape guys on the train . . ."

"They will know it was us," said Fred. "Especially if we have to go to court or something."

A car from the railroad pulled up beside the tracks. The train driver talked to someone in the passenger's seat and then headed to the front of the train.

"The train is going to leave in a minute," said Will. "What do we do?"

Now Fred looked as sick as Will had.

Officer Kronsky, a tall woman with short black hair, stepped out of the cruiser with the Maryland state flag on the door. She waved the boys over. Standing by the hood of the car, the officer took Fred's description of the boys running up the hill. She took Will's version. "Hmmmm."

Mr. Brown dropped his bag and stood at the back of the cruiser while Officer Kronsky asked more questions.

The train released its brakes with a blast of air and rumbled off down the tracks.

Officer Kronsky watched the train leave. She looked at the couple of flesh-colored pieces of shattered mannequin still on the tracks and shook her head.

"Idiots. If boys had half a brain, they would be really dangerous."

"What?" said Fred. Will could tell he was a little offended.

"Boys," said Officer Kronsky, flipping her notebook closed. "I see them doing stupid stuff every day. That poor driver thought he'd killed someone. All those people on the train are going to be late to work."

Officer Kronsky put her hat back on. "Boys sometimes aren't great at thinking through consequences."

Fred looked at the mannequin pieces on the white crushed stone. Fred looked down the tracks where their train to the field trip had disappeared. Fred looked at Will. They both nodded.

"Officer Kronsky," said Fred. "We did see something else that might help."

Officer Kronsky flipped her pad back open. She wrote down Fred and Will's description of the apes. She wrote down times, stops, everything Fred overheard.

"I'm glad you spoke up," said Officer Kronsky. "They might still be on the train." She got on her radio and told her partner to lock the train doors.

"Do you need any more from us?" asked Mr. Brown. The boys looked at him gratefully.

"This is plenty," said Officer Kronsky. "This is good. Really good." Officer Kronsky turned to Fred and Will. "Every once in a while I get a nice surprise on my job. You two guys are one of them. You want a lift to the next train stop? We can still get you to that field trip."

"That would be great," said Mr. Brown. "We can join up with our class."

Fred smiled. "And Will can join up with his new special friend."

Will couldn't help smiling.

But he still gave Fred a solid arm punch and told him, "Shut up."

GHOST VISION GLASSES
BY PATRICK CARMAN

Kyle Jennings was a normal ten-year-old kid when it came to his understanding of money. It was used, primarily, for three things:

- candy
- action figures
- weird stuff

Kyle was especially fond of weird stuff and would often limit his spending on candy and action figures in order to get more weird stuff. Some of the best weird stuff Kyle had included the following items:

- six cans of fart putty
- a magic trick that made it look like he'd cut his thumb off
- a Chia Head with a full head of green grass hair

231

(Probably Kyle's favorite weird thing, the Chia Head was pottery in the shape of a bald head, with tiny holes where green grass grew out like hair if you watered it regularly.)

- a camera that squirted water (nonoperational after recently attempted syrup squirt)
- a Magic 8 Ball
- a rubber chicken
- tennis shoes with wheels in them (one currently clogged with old chewing gum)

Kyle kept his stash of weird stuff in a plastic bin in his closet so Scotty Vincent wouldn't find it. Scotty Vincent was the biggest, meanest kid in the neighborhood. He had gigantic arms like a gorilla and always wore a bright orange baseball cap backward on his huge head.

And he liked to take Kyle's things.

For example, Kyle used to have a robot made out of grape soda cans until Scotty Vincent took it outside and crushed each can one at a time on the sidewalk in front of Kyle's house. (He started with the grape-soda-can head and worked his way down to the soda-can feet. It was disturbing.) And he'd once shown up with a pair of scissors and given the Chia Head a grass-hair crew cut, laughing the whole time.

Scotty Vincent's parents were just as bad, only larger and louder. They constantly yelled at Kyle to stay off their property, which was hard to do because they had a super-friendly horse named Skipper, tied up in their backyard, that would eat out of Kyle's hand.

"Get your hands away from that horse!" Scotty Vincent's mom often yelled. She was a large, obnoxious woman and she sometimes smelled like cheese. Scotty Vincent's dad, one of the hairiest and most unpleasant people Kyle had ever met, usually followed by throwing rotten fruit in Kyle's general direction and screaming, "This ain't no petting zoo!"

Scotty Vincent's parents ran some sort of mail-order internet business out of their house, so they were home quite a lot, which was probably why Scotty himself spent so much time outside during the summer months. Who'd want to stay indoors with those two all day?

At least Scotty's parents didn't go looking for kids to torment. That pursuit was Scotty's alone, and he did it well. He was not above knocking on Kyle's front door and acting all pleasant to Kyle's parents in order to gain access to his room, where Scotty proceeded to take whatever he wanted.

Sometimes, when no one was around, Kyle put on one of his fake mustaches and yelled out his bedroom window into the neighborhood, "Scotty Vincent, you're a big fat jerk!"

Then he shut the window very quickly and hid in his closet with all his weird things and his action figures and his candy.

It was there, on a particular summer day, that his father found him sleeping.

"Kyle," he said, pushing the sleeping boy with the toe of his tennis shoe. "Wake up. Time to go."

An hour later, after driving up into the mountains that surrounded the town Kyle lived in, the car pulled down a dirt drive and faced a tiny blue cabin. The cabin was old as dirt, but it had been a bargain his penny-pinching parents had long hoped for. Every previous summer they'd stayed at the lake they'd rented a place, but the winter had brought incredibly low prices, and Kyle's parents had purchased the little blue cabin. It was the crummiest, smallest cabin on Lake Lenore. The inside, Kyle assumed, would match the outside.

"This is it," said Kyle's mom, beaming with excitement. "Don't you just love it?"

"It's perfect," Kyle's dad agreed.

He slapped Kyle on the back and handed him the keys.

"Go ahead, you first."

It was early summer, a Saturday, and the lake was

brimming with kids. Unfortunately one of them was Scotty Vincent, who was just then pulling up to the dock jutting off the edge of the green grass. The big jerk had his own rowboat, which he'd rowed across the small lake with his gorilla arms. He wasted no time buttering up Kyle's mom and dad.

"I'm really glad you guys bought a place up here," Scotty said, although he couldn't help making a slightly sour face as he glanced at the cabin. He waved menacingly in Kyle's direction, but Kyle was already unlocking the door and hurrying inside.

The cabin smelled like old gym socks and, *wow*, was it small inside. Downstairs had a bedroom barely big enough for the double bed his parents would sleep on, a postage-stamp-sized kitchen, and a main room with a single couch and an ancient woodstove. At least there was a second floor, which Kyle went for immediately, in search of the attic room he'd be staying in.

The stairway to the second floor was narrow, with steps that creaked loudly under his feet. Upstairs was nothing but a small loft with a harrowingly low upside-down V-shaped ceiling. It was a head cracker for sure, so Kyle crawled along the floor.

"Awesome," he said. His imagination ran wild as he

thought about how he would transform the loft into a private lakeside fort. He'd create a Lake Lenore Scout Club and invite all his lake buddies to join. Their sworn duty would be to protect one another from Scotty Vincent and, if possible, sink his stupid rowboat.

Kyle set his backpack on the twin-size bed in the corner of the attic and took a good look around. There was a small window where he could see the lake past tall green fir trees, and in the shadowy far corner, something else.

"What's this?" he asked himself.

It was a cardboard box, and opening it up, Kyle found two things: a dead mouse and a stack of old comic books. He was sad for the mouse, but extremely happy otherwise, because he loved comic books.

"Whoa, these are old," he said, sitting down under the window where the light streamed in from outside. He held a thick stack of torn-up comics in his lap and started flipping pages. About five seconds later, he heard steps bolting quickly up the stairs. He put the stack of comics behind his back and leaned on them, holding them precariously against the wall of the loft.

"Nice place you got here."

His parents had let Scotty Vincent into the cabin, and he wasn't going to leave empty-handed.

"Find any treasures?"

Kyle squirmed on his butt, and the comics slid down on the wall a little bit.

"Nope, just this nice window here."

"What's in the box?" asked Scotty, crawling closer to Kyle, looking more like a gorilla than ever.

Kyle leaned harder against the wall as Scotty Vincent picked up the cardboard box and looked inside.

"Check that out!"

Kyle could see the wheels turning under Scotty's orange baseball cap. He could see that Scotty was thinking about picking up the dead mouse and dropping it down Kyle's shirt.

"You don't mind if I borrow this little guy, do you?"

Scotty Vincent laughed, picked up the mouse, and dropped it into the pocket of his T-shirt. He was, no doubt, imagining something terrible he could do with it, like scare some four-year-old kid half to death.

Scotty Vincent looked at Kyle very carefully.

"You sure you didn't find anything else up here?"

"Nope, nothing any good. Just dead mice and dust. And this nice window here."

"You're a weird kid, you know that?"

Kyle nodded enthusiastically as Scotty Vincent started

down the stairs. He turned at the last second and offered some advice accompanied by a wicked smile.

"Be careful out there on the water. It's pretty deep. You never know what might happen to a little kid like you."

Kyle was steaming mad as he peeked out the window and watched Scotty Vincent row away with a dead mouse in his pocket. He sat down under the window with the stack of old comics and started plowing through them, and quickly discovered it was much more of a treasure than he had first imagined.

They were all *Archie* comics from the year 1970, and this created an unfortunate bit of confusion for a ten-year-old like Kyle. The confusion was particularly strong when Kyle turned to pages filled with offers for the most incredible weird stuff Kyle had ever seen in his life. And what was even better—or so he thought—was how cheap everything was!

98 cents for a Hercules wristband!

79 cents for a handshake shocker!

49 cents for Vulcan ears!

$1.50 for an entire crime detection lab!

A 65-cent crazy-action billiard ball, 30-cent joke gum, and a magnet that lifted fifty pounds for a buck!

Kyle clutched the magazines to his chest, filled with a

warm sense of happiness. Could it really be true? Had he hit the weird-stuff jackpot? He ran downstairs and gathered up supplies: a handful of marshmallows for energy, a pad of paper, a pencil.

"Everything okay, sport?" asked his dad.

"Everything is great!" howled Kyle.

"Don't you want to go swimming in the lake?" his mother asked.

"Right after I get done setting up my room!" Kyle said.

An hour later Kyle had written down a grand total of twenty-seven weird items, including an air car, a secret pocket pen radio, a decoder ring, a werewolf mask, a dog whistle, a whoopee cushion, a trick baseball, and a family of sea monkeys. All that plus the wristband, hand shocker, Vulcan ears, crime detection lab, joke gum, magnet, and the crazy-action billiard ball and tons of other stuff, all for . . . for . . .

It couldn't be.

It was impossible.

But there it was, all in print in real comic books, so it had to be true!

All for only *seventeen dollars and twenty-seven cents*!

He'd done a lot of figuring to get the cost just right, because there was one item he wanted more than all the others, and it was expensive. He'd found the item in the very last comic on the very last page and known immediately that he had to have it. It was the one item in the old *Archie* comics that made him tingle with excitement.

Ghost Vision Glasses.

Putting them on made it possible to see real ghosts floating around right next to you! They were outrageously expensive—a whole ten dollars!—but wow, what an incredible weird item it was. The best weird item of them all.

He'd need a grand total of twenty-eight dollars, and while he couldn't be positive, he was nearly sure he had that much saved up back home.

Lake Lenore was up in the mountains, almost off the grid. If a person stood in the right spot (like in the tiny kitchen of the blue cabin) they could get a signal on a cell phone, but there was no mail service at the lake. He'd have to wait until he got home to place his orders.

A week at the lake moved like a slug on a wet tree: relentlessly slow. Kyle endured endless tormenting from Scotty Vincent, much of which revolved around getting into the lake. Scotty patrolled the perimeter in his dumb rowboat, seeking out other boys who dared to float along aimlessly on an inner tube. More than one kid had shared horrifying stories of being chased down, flipped over, and left for dead. Kyle wanted no part of that nonsense, and bore the ruthless heat of the week with cannonballs off the old boat dock and quick exits out of the cool water.

He pored over the order forms in the old comic books, double-checking his figures, changing the items a thousand times. But no matter how many times he adjusted his math, the expensive Ghost Vision Glasses were always at the top of the list.

At long last the week came to an end and Kyle, having nailed down the items he would buy with all of his saved money, closed the door to the blue cabin and raced his dad to the car. The second they pulled into the driveway back home, Kyle ran to his room and set the biggest weird-stuff buying spree of his young life in motion, which began by grabbing the sum total of his personal fortune: a jar of change, three gumballs, and some lint.

"Dad, I need paper money," he said, carrying his jar of pennies, nickels, dimes, and quarters into the kitchen. It was a big jar, filled to the rim, although as he peered inside the glass, there was an unfortunate amount of copper staring back. Lots and lots of pennies, mixed with a smaller number of nickels and dimes, and the occasional giant quarter.

"And if it's not asking too much, I'd like mostly ones, please. You can throw in a ten if that makes it easier," Kyle continued, thinking about the ten-dollar bill he was planning to send for the Ghost Vision Glasses.

Kyle's dad, always happy to see his son considering the idea of money at all and sensing a teaching moment in the making, poured the change out on the kitchen counter, where it appeared, sadly for Kyle, even more coppery than it did inside the jar.

"Start counting," said Kyle's dad. "I'll go get my wad of ones."

Kyle's dad was offensively thrifty, which was not to Kyle's advantage. At ten years old, he should have been getting at least twenty dollars a month for necessities, but he only got two crisp one-dollar bills a week. What he'd poured on the table was pocket change he obsessively collected from two primary sources:

Begging. Sometimes, if he begged just right after having gone through the checkout at Wal-Mart, his dad would have pity on Kyle and give him whatever came rolling back in the coin tray.

The ashtray in his mom's minivan, where she was in the habit of tossing nickels and dimes and pennies. It was their agreed-upon deal that whatever accumulated in the ashtray was Kyle's, so long as he took out the trash once every day.

It took the better part of what was left of Sunday to

count and stack all the change on the table, and when he was done, Kyle was disappointed to discover he had a little less than he'd expected: $28.11.

"Saving twenty-eight dollars takes discipline," Kyle's dad said. "I'm impressed!"

So impressed, it turned out, that Kyle's dad forked over twenty crisp one-dollar bills and a ten-dollar bill in exchange for all the coinage. True, it had also cost Kyle an additional fifteen minutes of his life, in which he was forced to endure a boring lecture on interest rates, savings, and the Federal Reserve, but still—thirty dollars! It meant he could afford every single thing on his list.

This turned out not to be true after Kyle calculated what it would cost for the stamps. There were eleven envelopes with eleven order forms asking for a total of twenty-seven weird things. Postage would run a whopping $4.84.

"Crud," said Kyle, and he went back to the drawing board with the comic books, refiguring the entire order. Somewhere between scratching the life-size raven's claw and adding back in the superstretchy monkey, Scotty Vincent appeared at his bedroom window. It was a hot day, and the window was slid open.

"Hot and boring," said Scotty Vincent. "Puts me in a bad mood."

Oh great, thought Kyle. As if Scotty Vincent in a good mood isn't bad enough.

"What the heck are you doing anyway?" asked Scotty Vincent.

"Nothing important," said Kyle. "Just being bored and hot, same as you."

Scotty started to push the first-story window farther open so he could climb through, as he was apt to do whenever he felt like it.

Kyle leaped for the window just as Scotty Vincent's flip-flop-clad foot landed on the sill. He was not usually one to slam a window shut, but Kyle really didn't want Scotty Vincent in his room checking out the incredible deals he was getting on weird stuff. His brain fired with thoughts of Scotty taking the order forms, the comics, the envelopes, the twenty crisp one-dollar bills and the ten!

And so it was that the window, which slid sideways, slammed into Scotty Vincent's flip-flop, which made Scotty Vincent scream, fall over into the yard, and begin flip-flopping around like a hooked fish on the dock at the lake. Kyle locked the window shut and pulled the blind, but it wasn't enough to protect him from hearing his tormentor yell as he hobbled toward the sidewalk and down the street.

"You are so toast, Kyle Jennings. *So* toast! You can't stay in there forever!"

And Scotty Vincent was right. If Kyle didn't get out of the house he couldn't buy stamps or mail the order forms for the incredible haul of weird stuff, and there was no way in a million years Kyle wasn't going to get those letters mailed. He got busy preparing the order forms, addressing the envelopes, and parsing out the funds. He was smart enough to know he couldn't mail coins—they were too heavy—so for items that were under a buck he put in an entire dollar bill with a note that said, "Please use the extra money I'm paying you to rush-deliver my order. Gratefully, Kyle Jennings."

The next morning Kyle ate a big breakfast and waited for his dad to leave for work and his mom to become hopelessly preoccupied with planning a Fourth of July family reunion at the new cabin. He waited until she was on the phone, talking to one of her four brothers.

"I'm going outside, be back later," he said.

His mom nodded, said something about staying away from the Vincents' horse, and waved him off. Instead of taking the normal route through the neighborhood, where he was sure to be spotted by Scotty Vincent, who would probably throw rocks at him or try to chase him down, Kyle went through the side door of the garage. He scaled the back fence, crept through the neighbors' shrubs, and emerged on a cul-de-sac he didn't know very well.

Two miles of walking and several close calls with dogs he'd never met before, and Kyle was back in his room, stamps purchased, letters mailed. He lay on his bed, basking in the glow of total awesomeness.

Soon, I will have twenty-seven of the best weird things money can buy.

It's a shame Kyle didn't understand two important facts of life:

Companies go out of business, especially ones that sell weird stuff.

Also, 1970 was a long time ago, and things had gotten a lot more expensive.

Four days.

Four days that felt like four years while Kyle waited for his weird stuff to show up.

Four days in which Scotty Vincent stopped by eleven times in order to convince Kyle's mom to let him into the house. It required precise coordination for Kyle to reach his mom just before Scotty knocked on the door so he could say, "Heading out through the garage, back in three hours!"

Four days.

That's how long it took for the mailbox to fill with a

stack of letters that nearly broke Kyle's heart. Every day he'd watched the mailbox like a hawk, running to the curb the second the mail carrier pulled away. And on the fourth day he found the stack of letters he'd sent out for all the weird stuff. There were horrible red stamped words on every one: RETURN TO SENDER, ADDRESSEE NOT FOUND.

He ripped open every letter and found that only one of the orders had not been returned.

The most expensive item of them all, a whole ten dollars. The Ghost Vision Glasses.

Kyle held out a tiny hope that the Ghost Vision Glasses order would go through, but he was so crestfallen in general he rode his bike at full speed to the Kmart at the edge of the neighborhood and blew all his money on candy and one action figure. Then he had the terrible luck of encountering Scotty Vincent on the way back home. Scotty was also on a bike, and Kyle knew better than to try and outrun the bigger, older kid.

"Give me the bag and we'll call it even," said Scotty Vincent.

Kyle felt he'd already endured about 80 percent of a disastrously bad day and trying to improve things for the better would only make it worse. So he handed over the bag of Kmart stuff (Nerds, Laffy Taffy, M&M's, a Captain America) and finished the ride home. At least he and Scotty Vincent were square and he could roam the neighborhood without being at the top of his hit list.

Day five produced considerably better news at the mailbox, although retrieving the news created another gorilla-size problem.

"Why are you always racing out here to check the mail as soon as it gets delivered?" asked Scotty Vincent, who had positioned himself behind a tree in the neighbor's yard. He began lumbering toward the mailbox at about the same rate that Kyle was walking down his driveway, and the two of them arrived at the curb simultaneously.

"My mom makes me bring in the mail and I like to get it over with so I can have my life back," said Kyle, a pretty good answer he'd come up with on the walk to the street.

"I don't believe you," said Scotty Vincent. "Something's up."

Scotty reached out his big gorilla-size claw of a hand and opened the mailbox door, reaching inside. To this day, Kyle doesn't know exactly why he slammed the door on Scotty Vincent's hand. Only that he had a feeling the Ghost Vision Glasses had arrived and he was terrified Scotty would take them and never give them back.

Scotty pulled his hand out and shook it, yelling something about how slamming his hand in the door was a really bad idea and Kyle was in big trouble and blah-blah-blah.

By the time Scotty got to the blah-blah-blah part, Kyle had already gotten his hands on what was in the mailbox and run halfway up the driveway toward the house. The last thing he heard was, "I'll get you!" before slamming the front door closed and realizing what he'd done.

Only a few days before, he'd shut Scotty Vincent's flip-flopped foot in a window. Now he'd slammed a mailbox door on the same kid's gorilla-size hand. In short, Kyle Jennings had officially made an enemy of the meanest, biggest kid in the neighborhood.

Kyle ran to his room and told his mom he didn't want to be bothered because he was right in the middle of reading *The Hobbit* and he was at a really good part with a dragon. This, he knew, would keep everyone away from his room, because it was rare for Kyle to read and when he did, his mother considered it a miracle that should not be tampered with. If Scotty Vincent came to the door acting all pleasant, she'd turn him away for sure.

Kyle double-checked the lock on his window and shut the blinds, then sat on his bed and looked at the letter. It was addressed to him, and instead of a return address, there was a drawing of a pair of glasses in the top left corner. He opened the envelope and pulled out a thick cream-colored card with words written delicately in black ink.

WE HAVE DELIVERED YOUR ORDER TO A SECURE
LOCATION. DO NOT UNDER ANY CIRCUMSTANCES
REMOVE PATENTED GHOST VISION GLASSES FROM
SAID SECURE LOCATION. REPEAT: DO NOT REMOVE
GHOST VISION GLASSES FROM ADDRESS PROVIDED ON
THE BACK OF THIS CARD. DOING SO IS CONSIDERED
EXTREMELY DANGEROUS.

Kyle turned the card over in his shaking fingers and read
the address.

BEHIND A VERY SMALL DOOR, ATTIC, THE LITTLE BLUE
CABIN, LAKE LENORE.

"They delivered my order to the cabin at the lake?" said
Kyle, a broad smile filling his face. "This is awesome!"

The smile on his face disappeared a moment later when
he heard Scotty Vincent tapping on the window outside.

"I hope you enjoy that book, because it's going to be
your last. You can't stay in there forever."

If Kyle had needed to wait more than one day to find the
Ghost Vision Glasses, it's scientifically possible that his
head might have exploded. He'd never been so excited in

his young life, not even when he knew he was getting a hamster on his fifth birthday. This was a whole different level of anticipation. So it was a lucky thing that the letter had arrived on a Friday at around noon and they were scheduled to leave for the cabin at 4:30 p.m. The only bad news was that Scotty Vincent and his terrible parents left an hour before Kyle did. When Kyle arrived at the blue cabin, Scotty Vincent was already sitting in his stupid rowboat, watching Kyle from the lake.

Kyle grabbed the keys and bolted for the cabin door before his parents got out of the car, and taking one last look back at the lake, he saw Scotty rowing toward the dock.

"I'm heading up to the attic so I can start this amazing book you got me!" said Kyle. His mother had gotten him a copy of the first Harry Potter book, which was fine except Kyle had seen the movie about a million times already. As he threw open the door he heard his mom say to his dad, "Look at our little reader—isn't it wonderful?"

Once Kyle was in the attic, he went back and forth between checking the tiny window and searching for anything that looked like a door. During the last visit he'd set up a beanbag to sit in and more or less decorated the space with paint and old cabin objects he'd found: wooden ducks, jars of junk, tattered Forest Service maps. He saw

Scotty Vincent arrive at the dock and tie up his crummy rowboat. He searched all along the ceiling for a trapdoor but found none. He went back to the window and saw that his mom and dad had told Scotty to come back later because of the important reading going on upstairs. He watched Scotty stare up at the window. He searched more frantically for a door, then took out the card and read the address once more.

BEHIND A VERY SMALL DOOR, ATTIC, THE LITTLE BLUE CABIN, LAKE LENORE.

"But there are no doors!" said Kyle, and he looked across the low upside-down-V ceiling again. He sat down, frustrated and angry, and looked at the Harry Potter book, which he'd kept in one hand for some unimaginable reason. He threw the book across the small room and watched as it hit the far corner by the floor.

"Everything okay up there?" his dad called from the kitchen.

"I'm good, just—um—I'm just settling in is all."

And he *was* good, because the book had hit something in the corner of the room, and that something had popped open.

"That Harry Potter kid really is magic," whispered Kyle.

When he'd crawled the length of the room and moved the book aside, Kyle found a door no bigger than his hand. He touched it with his fingers and flicked it open. Inside, darkness and cool air. He felt an unnatural chill, as if something unseen were watching him as he put his hand into the darkness and felt all around. At first he found nothing, but putting his whole arm in, he thought he felt something scurry across his hand. Kyle yanked his arm out, but not before taking hold of a box and dragging it along for the ride.

He shut the tiny door and ran to the window, where he saw Scotty Vincent rowing in the direction of two boys floating on inner tubes. Sitting down on the beanbag, Kyle examined the box more carefully. It was ancient wood, that much was for sure, and looking at it, he began to feel for the first time a little bit afraid. There were gold hinges and a velvet cord for a handle, and on the top, words burned in black:

THE GHOST VISION GLASSES.

This box alone is worth more than ten dollars, thought Kyle, as it crossed his mind to put it back where he'd found it and forget it had ever existed. But he was, above all things at that moment, curious. How could he not open the box and look inside?

And so he did.

There were no instructions, as he'd hoped there would be; only the glasses, which took his breath away. The frames were made of the same ancient wood as the box itself. But it was the lenses that made him gasp in wonder. They were iridescent, like the feathers on a certain kind of duck, and as he moved the glasses slowly back and forth, they seemed to pick up all sorts of images within the room that were not there.

He thought again about putting the box and the glasses back where he'd gotten them, and again his curiosity betrayed him. How could he open the box and not put them on? What if they worked? What if he actually saw a ghost? What then?

Picking them up, Kyle found the Ghost Vision Glasses were heavy and solid, as if they were made not of wood but marble. It was petrified wood, he decided, not unlike the bits and pieces that could be found strewn around the lake even now.

And then Kyle Jennings put the Ghost Vision Glasses on.

They were light as a feather resting on his nose, and they seemed to fit about as perfectly as a pair of glasses could. It was as if he didn't have them on at all. He might have thought just that, but for the change in what he saw with them on. The room, once bathed in dusty yellow light, turned an unnatural shade of watery green. He could still see the trail maps and the jars of nails and rusty bottle caps, but there was something more. Or, better said, there was someone else.

"You do realize no one has ordered a pair of those in over thirty years, don't you?" said the ghost. It was a man and it was old and it was staring down at Kyle. It leaned down closer, right up next to Kyle's face, and breathed fog into the air. Then it lifted its cape-covered arm and held it before Kyle's face.

It crossed Kyle's mind that this would probably be a great time to scream his head off, but for some reason, nothing would come out.

"You've got to keep them clean or you'll start to see all sorts of unexpected things," said the ghost, and he wiped his ghostly cape across the glasses. "There, that's better."

Kyle could see through the ghost to the wall on the other side as he sat down on a ghostly chair that appeared out of nowhere.

"The first rule about the glasses," said the ghost, "is that you can see and hear ghosts only when you're wearing them. Take them off and poof! I'll be gone."

Kyle slipped the glasses down on his nose and sure enough, the ghost was gone. Sliding them back up tight against his eyes made the ghost reappear with a vacant sort of smile on his face. "Who are you?" asked Kyle, surprised at the sound of his own voice.

"'Who was I?' is probably a better question."

"Okay, who were you then?" asked Kyle, feeling bolder and less afraid.

"I was a person who loved weird things as much as you do. I even sold weird things once. And sometimes I'd make things that I didn't tell anyone about."

"Like these glasses?"

"Maybe so," said the ghost, smiling silently. He shrugged and continued, "In my line of work I came across the very best weird stuff there ever was. It came with the territory. Why, I once owned a two-headed dog. And a thing that would blow up my hand like a balloon—great fun that was."

"You're kidding," said Kyle, and all he could think about as he looked at his own hand was how fun it would be to blow it up like a balloon and float away.

"No, no, I'm serious. There were many weird things. But the glasses—those are special. I kept them."

"So I see!" said Kyle, sitting up straighter in the beanbag. "But how did you get my letter if you're—you know . . ."

"Dead?"

"Yeah, dead."

"Being on the other side of a situation makes almost everything harder, but a few things are easier, like seeing when someone is trying to find you. Your order form was so very, very rare. Well, I just had to see you for myself. And so here I am and here you are."

"Yes, here we are," said Kyle, not knowing what else to say.

The ghost looked at Kyle for a long moment, turning his head sideways, as if he was a little nervous about asking. . . .

"What sort of weird things have you got in your collection?"

And then the two of them talked and talked about every weird thing either one of them had ever seen or found or hoped to get a hold of. They talked of slot machines, ventriloquist dummies, skeleton arms, and fake books with secret compartments.

"I once had a secret spy scope that could see through walls," said the ghost.

"Did not!"

"No seriously, I really did."

Night began to fall on the lake as they spoke, and the room grew dim.

"Your mother will be calling you to dinner before long," said the ghost. "So there's something important I must tell you right away. The second rule about the glasses, which is a bit of a secret among us ghosts, is that we can't do anything to you. You can see me and we can talk, but you don't have to worry. I can't affect the physical world, and neither can they."

"Who?" asked Kyle, but the ghost didn't answer him directly.

"I'd like to show you something."

"What is it? Is it something weird?"

"Come to think of it, I suppose it is," said the ghost, and he looked very seriously at Kyle for the first time since they'd met.

"Will you look out the window for me, just for a second? There's something I want you to see."

Kyle trusted the ghost and popped right up out of the beanbag. When he reached the window and looked outside, all the color drained out of his face and he thought again that he'd arrived at a pretty good moment to scream his head off. But again, he didn't, because the ghost came near and gently nudged Kyle back into his seat.

"I'm sorry you had to see that, but at least they were far away. They can't come in here. I won't let them."

"What were they?"

"Those were the bad ghosts. They were bad people in life and bad ghosts they have become. Just remember, they can be awfully mean and very scary to behold, but they can't harm you. Not in this life, anyway."

Kyle trembled where he sat as he thought of drawing the attention of what he'd seen hovering above the lake: more ghosts, but not the nice kind like the man in the room. They were ghouls and monsters with terrible faces and teeth and sunken eyes. They were the kind of ghosts that haunted.

"I'm what you might call a benevolent ghost," said the ghost. "I'm friendly, in other words. I mean you no harm. I rather like a little conversation, especially with someone that shares the same interests as I do. And as long as I'm here, those ghosts outside won't come in."

Kyle had to admit they had enjoyed a long and totally awesome conversation about the best things ever. Not a single second of it had been boring, scary, or stupid.

"So I shouldn't look outside," said Kyle. "I can do that. No problem."

"And more important, don't ever take the glasses out of this room. Here you're safe, but out there—well, they might not be able to hurt you, but they sure will scare you. We can't have the Ghost Vision Glasses out there."

"No problem!" said Kyle. "I'll just keep them in the cool box you made behind the little door, and whenever I come up here we can talk about weird stuff all day long! I'll even bring some of my best weird stuff so you can see it."

"You'd do that for me?"

"Totally!"

The ghost smiled at Kyle and it seemed genuinely happy.

"I'd very much enjoy seeing the Chia Head."

"Yeah, it's kind of amazing."

The ghost stood up and put his hand out as if to ask for the glasses.

"Time to put them away for now," he said. "But before you take them off, promise me you'll never take them out of this room."

"I promise," said Kyle, and he meant it. Nothing in the world could make him want to leave the safety of the attic with the glasses on. Not after the terrible things he'd seen floating over the lake.

"And one more thing," said the ghost as Kyle reached up to take off the glasses. "In case something happens and we don't see each other again, I had a marvelous time talking to you. You're very interesting."

"Ditto," said Kyle, and he took off the Ghost Vision Glasses, which felt heavy in his hands.

The ghost was gone and seemed to have otherworldly good timing, because Kyle's dad came up the stairs a few seconds later.

"Wow, you really like it up here, huh?" he asked.

"I do, Dad, a lot."

"Well, I'm glad. Now come down here and get some dinner—I'm barbecuing hamburgers!"

"Be right down."

Kyle's dad looked more closely at the room, taking in the decorations and the thing Kyle held in his hand.

"Cool glasses," his dad said.

"Um—yeah, they are. I found them up here. Can I keep them?"

"Sure you can keep them. Whatever was in the cabin when we got here is ours now, including the giant spider under the kitchen sink."

"You're kidding."

"I wish. Now come on, we've got some burgers to eat."

Kyle could tell his dad was in one of his moods where it was time to go and stalling wasn't going to be a good idea, so he set the Ghost Vision Glasses carefully on the bean-bag and followed his dad down the narrow stairs. He took a quick look back, longing to wear them again, and then he was downstairs in the tiny kitchen, where his mom was yammering on her cell phone with someone.

"Well, the thing is, we hadn't really planned on it," she said.

Kyle looked at his dad but he just shrugged. He didn't know who she was talking to.

"Of course I understand. Kyle has been a reading fool

here lately, and I'm sure they miss seeing each other. He just loves books."

Kyle's mom beamed with pride about the reading of the books and looked out toward the lake.

"Oh, there you are! I see you now. How did you get lights on a rowboat? Impressive!"

She hung up the phone and looked at Kyle's dad.

"You didn't," he said.

"Well, sure I did. They're not that bad."

"They keep a horse tied to a rope in their backyard and they're loud and obnoxious," my dad said.

"Better keep it down, they're almost here."

Kyle's mom took him by the shoulders and basically forced him out the door and onto the front lawn, where a cruddy old rowboat was coming to a stop at the cabin's dock.

"Oh no," said Kyle.

Scotty Vincent and his parents were all getting out of the boat. Kyle wondered how they'd all gotten in the boat without sinking it. They were a chunky bunch, and the boat wasn't that big. His second thought was that he absolutely, positively had to sit as far away from Scotty as humanly possible.

"Hi, Kyle!" said Scotty in the most sugary-sweet, disgusting voice Kyle had ever heard. "How the heck are you?"

"Yeah, same here," said Kyle, which made no sense

whatsoever, but that was par for the course when he was within ten feet of a bully.

"You're like the funniest guy ever!" said Scotty Vincent, but the second the parents turned to talk to one another, his expression said, *Har har har, you know what's funny? Me kicking you really hard under the table while we sit with your dumb parents.*

Dinner was going about as expected for Kyle, with the Vincents being super loud and annoying while they talked about their mail-order business and the gigantic cabin they owned on the other side of the lake and a bunch of other humongously boring stuff that made Kyle's dad look longingly at the sun setting behind the trees. Scotty kicked Kyle under the table hard enough that Kyle snorted Pepsi down the wrong pipe and had to walk off into the trees in order to spit, cough, and blow his nose. When he came back, Scotty Vincent was gone.

"Where'd Scotty go?" asked Kyle, staring off toward the rowboat with its ring of Christmas lights around the edge. He had to admit the boat looked pretty boss with the lights and all. But Scotty wasn't there.

"He went inside to get more ketchup," said Mr. Vincent. "The boy does love ketchup!" he howled, laughing noisily for no particular reason.

"Ketchup?" was all Kyle could say, his voice soft under the bellowing voice of Mrs. Vincent repeating her husband like a parrot and every bit as loudly, "The boy does love ketchup!"

Kyle sat down at the table nervously, waiting for Scotty to appear at the door of the blue cabin, wondering what was taking so long. But then Scotty popped out of the sliding door with a fresh bottle of ketchup in his hand, holding it up like a trophy, all smiles.

"Found it!" he yelled, and his parents laughed and pointed. They were odd that way, always laughing annoyingly at unfunny things.

The rest of the dinner party crawled by as Kyle thought about the ghost and the glasses and wished a thousand times that the Vincents would get in their boat and row away and never come back. All Kyle really wanted to do was return to the attic, put on the Ghost Vision Glasses, and talk about weird stuff.

Finally Mr. Vincent lifted his giant butt off the picnic bench and stretched out his arms, which, apparently, was some sort of signal.

When I get up and stretch, everyone start getting ready to go. Got it?

It must have been true because Mrs. Vincent got up

and started thanking my mom profusely and asking her to come over with the whole family the next night, while Scotty Vincent headed for the boat without saying a word to anyone. He was not, generally speaking, a thankful kid. And his parents didn't seem to care because they didn't tell him to come back and thank my parents for the dinner, while Mr. Vincent slapped my dad on the back and said, "A little overcooked on those burgers, but the ketchup helped!" and laughed and laughed with Mrs. Vincent.

Kyle watched them get into the boat, a process that required a fair amount of time-consuming coordination between the three of them, and then he turned to go inside the blue cabin.

"See ya later," said Scotty Vincent, sensing Kyle's imminent departure before his own. "And hey—I like the beanbag. That thing is pretty comfortable."

Kyle's parents took no notice of the comment, but it hit Kyle like a punch in the gut. He started backpedaling toward the cabin, staring at Scotty, who was just taking hold of the oars as his parents got situated.

Through the tiny front room and the tinier kitchen, around the corner and up the narrow stairs, and right up next to the beanbag, Kyle hoped against all hope that the Ghost Vision Glasses would still be there. He saw the box first, forgetting that he'd left the glasses sitting loose on the beanbag, and for a flash of a second he felt relieved. But then he opened the box and remembered he hadn't put them inside and, searching all around, found no sign of the Ghost Vision Glasses.

Kyle's first thought was, surprisingly, less about how mad he was that Scotty Vincent had taken such a treasured item, and more about what a catastrophe it was that the glasses were outside the room.

What had the ghost said?

Don't ever take the glasses out of this room. Here you're safe, but out there—well, they might not be able to hurt you, but they sure will scare you. We can't have the Ghost Vision Glasses out there.

Kyle ran to the small, square window and peered out. The rowboat had only just started wobbling away. The sun had set and the string of lights cast a glow on Scotty Vincent's face as he looked up at Kyle and smiled.

Scotty stopped rowing and put his hand in the pocket of his pants. He held up the Ghost Vision Glasses so Kyle could see them, smiling wickedly at what he'd done. He held them over the water, as if to drop them overboard.

"Yeah, do that!" Kyle yelled, but the window was closed and Scotty couldn't hear him. "Just don't put them on!"

But it was no use. Scotty Vincent held the glasses between

his teeth and began rowing again as Kyle ran down the stairs, through the cabin, and out onto the grass. By the time he reached the dock in front of his lawn, the rowboat was twenty feet away and Scotty Vincent was laughing as he put the Ghost Vision Glasses on.

"This is bad," Kyle said quietly. His dad came up alongside him.

"They're kind of an annoying family, aren't they?" he said, and right when he did, Scotty Vincent started to freak out.

He turned as pale as a sheet, looking above and around himself as if something awful was coming near.

"There's one on your shoulder!" cried Scotty Vincent, and his arm windmilled wide and fast, slapping his mother on the shoulder and sending her flying out of the boat and into the water.

"Scotty! What on earth!" said Scotty's dad, but that was no use, as Scotty apparently saw another ghost attacking Mr. Vincent. Scotty screamed, picked up both of his feet, and kicked his dad right in the middle of his huge gut. Mr. Vincent did a pretty nice backward somersault off the bow and came up gasping for air.

"This is getting weird," said Kyle's dad. Kyle's mom had joined them as well, and she seemed more perplexed than concerned.

"Should we go in after them?"

"I don't think so," said Kyle's dad. "Maybe it's a family game or something. What else could it be?"

Scotty Vincent was standing up in the boat, waving his arms like a maniac, punching at the air, and spinning in circles. He came to a sudden stop as his mother yelled from the water.

"Scotty Vincent! What has gotten into you?"

Scotty looked at his mother in the water and must have seen a ghostly trout or, more likely, a ghost zombie trying to pull his mom under.

"Don't move, Mom! I'll save you!"

And with that, Scotty Vincent dove off the rowboat and landed a ten-point belly flop about a foot away from his mom's head.

"I'm not sure we should take them up on dinner at their place," said Kyle's mom. "They're starting to freak me out a little bit."

"A wise idea," said Kyle's dad.

When Scotty Vincent popped up out of the water, his dad was already making the monstrous effort to get back into the boat, with modest success. It took four or five tries to throw himself over the edge, his chest heaving as though he'd run a marathon by the time he'd gotten on board. He hoisted Mrs. Vincent into the boat with one great pull of his arms, and chose to leave his son in the water.

"Grab the rope, but you're not coming back in here!" yelled Mr. Vincent. He was just as loud as ever, but he sure wasn't laughing anymore as he started rowing away, muttering with his wife about what in the world had gotten into their boy. Kyle was pretty sure he heard Mrs. Vincent say something about the food they'd eaten as she glared back at Kyle and his family, who stood gaping at the lake, unable to speak.

Kyle's parents were dumbstruck by the weirdness of it all, but Kyle was unable to speak for an entirely different reason.

The Ghost Vision Glasses were gone. They'd fallen off Scotty's face in the wake of a monster belly flop. And they were heavy. And the lake was deep, like fifty feet.

It was all Kyle could do not to cry or scream or dive in after the Ghost Vision Glasses. But he just stood there, unable to move, as the coolest weird thing he'd ever owned came to rest at the bottom of Lake Lenore.

There were many bummers about that first summer in which Kyle stayed at the blue cabin his parents had purchased. He'd spent all his money on candy and a Captain

America action figure that Scotty Vincent took from him. He didn't get a single new weird item for his collection. And by far the worse thing of all, the Ghost Vision Glasses—which he'd only had for a grand total of about two hours—had sunk to the bottom of a fifty-foot-deep lake.

On the upside, Kyle learned some valuable lessons about how money works, found some awesome old comic books, and got to spend weekends at a nifty new cabin where he made a lot of new friends. And best of all by a country mile? Scotty Vincent stopped acting like a jerk, not just to Kyle, but to every kid in the neighborhood and every kid up at the lake. Whatever he'd seen in the Ghost Vision Glasses had set him straight for good, so much so that he even returned the Captain America action figure and let Kyle feed the horse whenever he wanted to.

In the end, Kyle was sad that he'd never have the chance to talk to the ghost at the blue cabin again, and a little bummed that he couldn't say thank you. He did the best he could on the last Sunday of the summer at the cabin. Sitting in the attic, he said thanks.

"Thanks for the amazing conversation about weird stuff," said Kyle. He had brought his Chia Head, which was in full green bloom. He held it up, hoping the ghost could see it. "And thank you, thank you, thank you for making Scotty Vincent a better kid. It means a lot."

"Come on, Kyle! We gotta go," yelled Kyle's dad from downstairs. Kyle set the Chia Head on the floor in the middle of the small room so the ghost would have some company while he was gone. A few minutes later they were driving away, waving to the lake and looking forward to seeing it again soon.

When they got home there was a letter in the mailbox, just like the one Kyle had gotten with the attic address. Inside, a card with a message on it:

YOU'RE WELCOME. AND THANK YOU FOR THE WEIRD COMPANY!

Kyle went into his room and set the card inside the bin with all of his other weird stuff. He closed the bin and pulled the blinds to his room, letting the sunshine in.

"Hey, little man."

Kyle swung around and found his dad standing in the doorway with a cardboard box. "You'll never guess what I found in the attic."

Kyle's dad set the box on the floor.

"After you found those old *Archie*s up at the cabin, I remembered."

Kyle's dad reached in and took an inch-thick pile out of the box. "My old superhero comic books!" he said, grinning from ear to ear. "I used to love these things. Too bad I didn't take better care of them. Probably not worth much, but they sure are fun to look at."

Kyle practically dove from the window to the door, landing on his knees, where he dug into the box and found piles of 1970s *Hulk*, *Captain America*, and *Fantastic Four* issues.

"These are awesome!" said Kyle. "Can I keep them?"

"Sure you can," said his dad. "Maybe we can take them up to the cabin next time we go and add them to the others."

As Kyle's dad turned to leave, Kyle sat down on his bed and started flipping the pages of a *Fantastic Four* issue with tattered corners and yellowed pages.

The sun warmed the room and a soft breeze ruffled the pages of the comic.

He was thinking weird thoughts.

If Archie and Jughead can lead me to a pair of Ghost Vision Glasses, imagine what the Hulk and Captain America can do. I'll have my very own superpower before the week is out!

And he was right.

ABOUT
GUYS READ

Guys Read mysterious stuff. And you just proved it. (Unless you just opened the book to this page and started reading. In which case, we feel bad for you because you missed some pretty thrilling stuff.)

Now what?

Now we keep going—Guys Read keeps working to find good stuff for you to read, you read it and pass it along to other guys. Here's how we can do it.

For ten years, Guys Read has been at www.guysread.com, collecting recommendations of what guys really want to read. We have gathered recommendations of thousands of great funny books, scary books, action books, illustrated books, information books, wordless books, sci-fi books, mystery books, and you-name-it books.

So what's your part of the job? Simple: Try out some of the suggestions at guysread.com, try some of the other stuff written by the authors in this book, then let us know what you think. Tell us what you like to read. Tell us what you don't like to read. The more you tell us, the more great book recommendations we can collect. It might even help us choose the writers for the next installment of Guys Read.

Thanks for reading

And thanks for helping Guys Read.

JON SCIESZKA (editor) is the author of numerous picture books, middle grade series, and even a memoir. From 2007–2010 he served as the first National Ambassador for Children's Literature, appointed by the Library of Congress. Jon is actively promoting his interest in getting boys to read through his Guys Read initiative and website. He lives in Brooklyn with his family. Visit him online at www.jsworldwide.com and at www.guysread.com.

SELECTED TITLES

THE TRUE STORY OF THE THREE LITTLE PIGS
(Illustrated by Lane Smith)

THE STINKY CHEESE MAN AND
OTHER FAIRLY STUPID FAIRY TALES
(Illustrated by Lane Smith)

The Time Warp Trio series
(Illustrated by Lane Smith)

M. T. ANDERSON ("The Old, Dead Nuisance") has written picture books for children, adventure novels for young readers, and several books for older readers. The first volume of his Octavian Nothing saga won the National Book Award and the *Boston Globe–Horn Book* Award. He lives in Boston. Find him online at www.mt-anderson.com.

SELECTED TITLES

FEED

BURGER WUSS

THE ASTONISHING LIFE OF OCTAVIAN NOTHING,
TRAITOR TO THE NATION, VOLUME I: THE POX PARTY

PATRICK CARMAN ("Ghost Vision Glasses") is the author of the bestselling Skeleton Creek, The Land of Elyon, and Atherton series. He pioneered the concept of vbooks—books that have online video components—and has visited hundreds of classrooms via Skype and webcam. He lives in Walla Walla, Washington. Find out more at www.patrickcarman.com.

SELECTED TITLES

The Skeleton Creek series, including
GHOST IN THE MACHINE

THE BLACK CIRCLE—The 39 Clues, Book 5

DARK EDEN

GENNIFER CHOLDENKO ("The Snake Mafia") was the youngest of four kids in her family. As a result, her childhood nicknames were Snot-Nose, Short Stuff, and Shrimp. Gennifer's book AL CAPONE DOES MY SHIRTS received a Newbery Honor. Gennifer lives in the San Francisco Bay Area. You can visit her online at www.choldenko.com.

SELECTED TITLES

AL CAPONE DOES MY SHIRTS

IF A TREE FALLS AT LUNCH PERIOD

NO PASSENGERS BEYOND THIS POINT

MATT DE LA PEÑA ("Believing in Brooklyn"), also known as Matt "No D" la Peña, grew up in a surf town on the coast of California, where the main thing on his mind was basketball. He won a scholarship to the University of the Pacific, where he helped his team reach the Division I Tournament. Now Matt lives in New York, where he writes and teaches creative writing at New York University. You can find out more at www.mattdelapena.com.

SELECTED TITLES

BALL DON'T LIE

MEXICAN WHITEBOY

WE WERE HERE

MARGARET PETERSON HADDIX ("Thad, the Ghost, and Me") is the author of the bestselling Missing series and the Shadow Children series. She grew up on a farm between two small towns and comes from a long line of farmers and a long line of bookworms. She lives in Ohio. Visit her online at www.haddixbooks.com.

SELECTED TITLES

The Shadow Children Series, including

AMONG THE HIDDEN

DOUBLE IDENTITY

INTO THE GAUNTLET—The 39 Clues, Book 10

BRUCE HALE ("Nate Macavoy, Monster Hunter") was raised by wolves just outside of Los Angeles. He has written and illustrated more than twenty-five books for kids, including the Edgar Award–nominated Chet Gecko Mystery series. Bruce lives in Southern California. You can find him online at www.brucehale.com.

SELECTED TITLES

The Chet Gecko Mystery series, including
HISS ME DEADLY

The Underwhere series, including
PRINCE OF UNDERWHERE
(Illustrated by Shane Hillman)

SNORING BEAUTY (Illustrated by Howard Fine)

ANTHONY HOROWITZ ("The Double Eagle Has Landed") grew up in England surrounded by wealth and mystery. He found his escape in the novels and movies of James Bond, and they inspired him to create his famous character Alex Rider. Anthony's mother gave him a human skull for his thirteenth birthday. He lives in England, and you can find him online at www.anthonyhorowitz.com.

SELECTED TITLES

The Alex Rider Adventures, including SCORPIA RISING

The Diamond Brothers Mysteries, including
I KNOW WHAT YOU DID LAST WEDNESDAY

JARRETT J. KROSOCZKA ("Pudding") is an international supersecret agent spy. After falling into a vat of toxic waste, Jarrett was endowed with the ability to fly, shoot laser beams out of his eyes, and run at lightning speed. When not keeping the world safe from evil space dinosaurs, Jarrett enjoys writing and illustrating books. Only one of these things is true. You can find out which at www.studiojjk.com.

SELECTED TITLES

The Lunch Lady graphic novel series, including
LUNCH LADY AND THE BAKE SALE BANDIT

MAX FOR PRESIDENT

PUNK FARM

WALTER DEAN MYERS ("Pirate") is a children's book legend. He grew up in New York, and dropped out of high school to join the army on his seventeenth birthday. A teacher who knew he was going to drop out of school made him promise to keep writing no matter what happened to him. Walter lives in Jersey City, New Jersey. Visit him online at www.walterdeanmyers.net.

SELECTED TITLES

LOCKDOWN

MONSTER

BAD BOY: *A Memoir*

JAMES PATTERSON ("Boys Will Be Boys") is one of the bestselling authors of all time. His books for children include the Daniel X series, the Maximum Ride series, and the Witch & Wizard series. He is also the founder of the literacy initiative and website, ReadKiddoRead. James lives Connecticut. Find out more at www.jamespatterson.com.

SELECTED TITLES

The Daniel X Series, including

THE DANGEROUS DAYS OF DANIEL X

The Maximum Ride Series, including ANGEL

MIDDLE SCHOOL, THE WORST YEARS OF MY LIFE

BRETT HELQUIST (Illustrator) loved to read comic strips when he was little. Since then, Brett has illustrated many bestselling books, including CHASING VERMEER by Blue Balliett. Brett lives in Brooklyn, New York. Visit him online at www.bretthelquist.com.

SELECTED TITLES

A Series of Unfortunate Events, including

THE BAD BEGINNING
(written by Lemony Snicket)

ROGER, THE JOLLY PIRATE

THE THREE MUSKETEERS
(written by Alexander Dumas)

SOME PEOPLE JUST CAN'T TELL A JOKE.
THOSE PEOPLE ARE NOT IN THIS BOOK.

GUYS†READ

FUNNY BUSINESS

EDITED BY
JON SCIESZKA

Book One in the Guys Read Library of Great Reading